HUNTER'S MISSION

BROTHERHOOD PROTECTORS WORLD

TEAM EAGLE
BOOK TWO

KENDALL TALBOT

Twisted Page Press LLC

BROTHERHOOD PROTECTORS

ORIGINAL SERIES BY ELLE JAMES

Brotherhood Protectors Series

Montana SEAL (#1)

Bride Protector SEAL (#2)

Montana D-Force (#3)

Cowboy D-Force (#4)

Montana Ranger (#5)

Montana Dog Soldier (#6)

Montana SEAL Daddy (#7)

Montana Ranger's Wedding Vow (#8)

Montana SEAL Undercover Daddy (#9)

Cape Cod SEAL Rescue (#10)

Montana SEAL Friendly Fire (#11)

Montana SEAL's Mail-Order Bride (#12)

SEAL Justice (#13)

Ranger Creed (#14)

Delta Force Rescue (#15)

Dog Days of Christmas (#16)

Montana Rescue (#17)

Montana Ranger Returns (#18)

BROTHERHOOD PROTECTORS WORLD

ORIGINAL SERIES BY ELLE JAMES

Brotherhood Protectors Colorado World
Team EAGLE

Booker's Mission - Kris Norris
Hunter's Mission - Kendall Talbot
Gunn's Mission - Delilah Devlin
Xavier's Mission - Lori Matthews
Wyatt's Mission - Jen Talty

Team Raptor

Darius' Promise - Jen Talty
Simon's Promise - Leanne Tyler
Nash's Promise - Stacey Wilk
Spencer's Promise - Deanna L. Rowley
Logan's Promise - Kris Norris

Team Falco

Fighting for Esme - Jen Talty
Fighting for Charli - Leanne Tyler
Fighting for Tessa - Stacey Wilk
Fighting for Kora - Deanna L. Rowley
Fighting for Fiona - Kris Norris

Athena Project
Beck's Six - Desiree Holt

Victoria's Six - Delilah Devlin
Cygny's Six - Reina Torres
Fay's Six - Jen Talty
Melody's Six - Regan Black

Team Trojan
Defending Sophie - Desiree Holt
Defending Evangeline - Delilah Devlin
Defending Casey - Reina Torres
Defending Sparrow - Jen Talty
Defending Avery - Regan Black

Brotherhood Protectors Yellowstone World
Team Wolf
Guarding Harper - Desiree Holt
Guarding Hannah - Delilah Devlin
Guarding Eris - Reina Torres
Guarding Payton - Jen Talty
Guarding Leah - Regan Black

Brotherhood Protectors Yellowstone World
Team Eagle
Booker's Mission - Kris Norris
Hunter's Mission - Kendall Talbot
Gunn's Mission - Delilah Devlin
Xavier's Mission - Lori Matthews
Wyatt's Mission - Jen Talty

CHAPTER 1

LAYLA

WHEN I'D FINALLY RECEIVED my funding to take my botany research work to the Amazon jungle, I'd expected torrential rain, extreme heat, and stifling humidity. What I hadn't anticipated was having a creep for a boss. Neville Parker thought he was God's gift to women.

He fucking wasn't. Fifty-five-year-old Neville was good-looking; I would give him that. But it was difficult to see how handsome he was when the bastard was always making crass remarks and trying to peer down my top.

But while it was great that he wasn't here ogling me, it was also annoying. We should be working together as a team. But I use the word team loosely. For months now, Cody, my lab assistant, and I had been doing all the work while Neville had been doing . . . I have no idea what he actually did while we

1

traipsed through the jungle all day. Then again, he still had two more years left on his research tenure, so he could afford to be lazy, I couldn't.

I stepped over the moss-covered log, and my rubber boot squelched into ankle-deep mud on the other side. "It's really muddy this way. Be careful." I turned to Cody. He was a brilliant scientist and had amazing language skills, but traipsing through the jungle was not one of his superpowers.

"I'm good." He reached for a vine that crossed over the log. His long legs straddled the dead tree that, based on the dense moss covering the trunk, must have fallen over decades ago. Or maybe even hundreds of years ago.

A pungent stench overpowered the usual jungle aromas of mud and leaves, and my empty stomach churned. "Ugh, what's that smell?" I covered my nose with my sleeve.

"Must be a dead animal around here somewhere." Cody's voice was muffled behind his hand.

As I peered into the gnarly underbrush, searching for a rotting carcass, the lush jungle enveloped me. The air amongst the overgrown vegetation was always thick like it was dense with the abundance of natural aromas. On my first trek into the jungle, I'd struggled to breathe. Over the last eleven months, I'd become used to the thick air. I'd even grown to love it. It was going to be damn hard to return to my hometown of Yellowstone,

Wyoming. Hopefully, that won't be for a few more years.

Time was ticking, though. Unless I could stabilize my formula for my burns ointment, the plug was going to be pulled on my funding, and our entire research project would be boxed up and likely never seen again. But despite trying damn hard, I still needed conclusive proof of a viable product, and I only had seven months left to prove my natural ointment worked.

Tick. Tick. Tick.

Everywhere I looked was green: plants, giant leaves, enormous trees, and strangler figs and vines that tied it all together in a living macramé. I often had to pinch myself to confirm I really was in the Amazon jungle. But as much as it was amazing, it was also terrifying. Without my compass, getting lost was a certainty. There were no buildings, roads, or paths, and the direction we'd chosen to scout today didn't seem to have animal tracks.

Today's rain had cleared a couple of hours ago, but it would take weeks of sunshine to dry up the thick mud and puddles covering the forest floor. Or maybe it never dried up in this area of the forest. It wouldn't surprise me; it rained a lot in the Amazon.

I wiped the sweat from my brow and sliced my machete through the underbrush. A thorny vine grabbed the sleeve of my shirt like desperate fingers warning me not to go any farther.

"That smell is getting worse." Cody made a gagging noise.

"I know. I don't think I've smelled death out here before." I paused next to a tree with a trunk as wide as the car I'd sold before I left home, the stench lingering in the stifling air.

The odor didn't worry me; death was natural. What worried me was what had killed the animal. The Amazon has its share of lethal creatures, six of which could fit in the palm of my hand. But it was the jaguar that I feared the most. I hadn't seen one in the flesh yet, but I'd heard one, and that was terrifying enough.

"Keep your eyes open, Cody." I tried to peer through the field of green, but it was impossible. "There's no telling what might be out here."

"You got your gun handy?" he asked.

I tapped my thigh holster strapped over my cargo pants. "Sure do."

I hadn't had to shoot an animal yet; I hoped I wouldn't have to shoot one today.

Cody didn't have a gun. I'd seen his target practice and it was safer for both of us that he wasn't armed.

I checked my watch. *Damn it.* We'd been out here for three hours already, and we hadn't seen, let alone harvested, any Inocea berries. Each time we went in search of my precious ingredient, which was only known to grow in this region of the Amazon, we had to venture farther away from the river and deeper into the jungle. Trekking this bush was both time-consuming and frustrating, especially considering the berries seemed so abundant when I'd first set up my jungle laboratory.

Wild screeches filled the air, giving me a slight reprieve from the suffocating silence surrounding us. Up to my ankles in mud, I paused, searching for movement amidst the towering trees.

"There they are." Cody pointed to the canopy behind us, where a group of monkeys scampered from branch to branch.

Their ear-splitting chorus dominated everything, and it would be easy to believe those monkeys were the kings of the jungle. They weren't; that moniker was reserved for the jaguar.

"I could watch them every day." Cody grinned so wide he had to adjust his glasses off his cheeks.

"Amazing, aren't they?" I watched their acrobatics with a hint of envy. It would be amazing to be so free. Free of responsibilities. Free of guilt.

"Sure are. When I die, I'm coming back as a spider monkey," he yelled over their ruckus.

I laughed. "So you believe in reincarnation, huh? I didn't know that about you."

"Sure. Haven't you seen The Lion King? You know, circle of life and all that." He puffed out his chest like he'd bestowed some divine logic upon me.

I didn't have the heart to tell him that the circle of

life meant that one creature's death gave new life to another.

"What would you come back as?" Cody wiped the sweat from his brow with his sleeve cuff.

Anything that couldn't injure a sibling. Avoiding the pointless conversation, I said, "Come on, let's do twenty more minutes before we turn around. This area is fruitless."

"I see what you did there . . . boom, boom." Chuckling, he patted my shoulder. "Hey, it's okay, we'll find more berries. We have to. They were everywhere when we first arrived."

"I know." I hooked my thumbs into the shoulder straps of my pack and forged ahead.

With each step, the sounds of the monkeys were absorbed by the eerie whispers of vegetation. The stillness was as if every living organism around us was holding its breath, waiting for our demise.

As I hacked at a pair of vines that had twisted into knots as they stretched the distance between two enormous trees, I couldn't halt my swirling thoughts over the consequences of our presence in this fragile ecosystem.

Will the native tribes suffer because of our intrusion?

Am I disrupting the balance of nature in my pursuit of a medical miracle?

Is my quest a complete waste of time and money?

Questions without answers reminded me of the weight of my responsibility. So many people relied on my project being a success, including Cody and Neville. Neville had been here much longer than me, and I'd been lucky that he was willing to share the plant research he'd done before I'd arrived, or I wouldn't be as far along as I was.

In the jungle, there was no such thing as sunrise or sunset. Sunlight rarely penetrated the dense canopy and the forest floor lived in almost eternal dimness. Occasionally, a spear of sunlight would beam down from the sky like a finger of God, and tiny particles would dance in the glow like they were having a party.

There were no spears of light at the moment. No dancing particles. No breezes carrying luscious scents of virgin rainforest. Instead, we were surrounded by an extreme stillness, and with every pace the rotten stench increased in intensity.

"Maybe we should head back. It's getting late." My shoulders slumped. Another day wasted.

"Let's just go a bit farther." He rested his hand on my arm and shoved around me to take the lead. "I have a feeling we're close."

Cody's determination mirrored my own. Except while my drive was to improve the suffering of burn victims, Cody wanted to demonstrate that his chosen career path was worth the money invested by his parents in his education. He felt he had to pay back more than just their financial contribution; he wanted them to be proud of him. He'd never said as much, but every time he spoke to them on our satellite phone, I heard the longing in his tone.

The scent of decay still clung to the air, and I tried to ignore both the foul odor and my stupid thoughts that something could be stalking us. In the jungle, something was always watching. It was just potluck whether or not that spectator was friendly.

I had to focus on my mission and find those berries. Burns victims needed my ointment.

Pushing away my doubts and fears, I trudged after Cody. He seemed to make easy work of the mud that stuck to our boots like epoxy.

At five-foot-five, I wasn't short, and I wasn't tall, but I had long legs and a short torso.

When I'm older, my boobs will probably sag so much they'll flank my belly button.

Now that's an image I didn't need.

Not that I had to worry. Nobody had seen me naked in years, and nobody was lining up to see me naked now. *Except Neville.* I would rather pull my pubes out one by one than undress in front of that creep.

My stomach rumbled, and Cody flicked his gaze at me over his shoulder. "Jeez, Layla, that was loud enough to attract the black caimans."

I laughed. "I know. I'm starving. What are the chances that Neville has dinner on the go?"

"Zero to zilch."

"Yeah, that's what I thought." Neville should be

helping us search for the berries instead of pretending he had a stomachache. If anyone could win a Pulitzer for journalling a plethora of excuses, it would be Neville fucking Parker.

"There! I see some." Cody pointed at a cluster of Inocea berries to our right. Their deep red hue stood out against the large verdant leaves of the Inocea bush.

"Thank you, Amazon gods." I swept my gaze skyward just in time to witness a toucan with a bright orange beak land on a branch above us. I reached for my camera. *Damn, I didn't bring it.* Then again, I probably already had two hundred photos of toucans from just the first three months of my posting down here.

Aiming for our prize, Cody climbed over the gnarly bushes like a stalk. I barged through them like a bulldozer.

Cody had sliced off a bunch of berries by the time I reached him. The berries grew like grapes in compact bunches, and seemed to flourish at a height that was just beyond my reach. Lucky for me, Cody was both tall and a willing participant in my research.

"Finally," I said as I stepped beside him. I peeled my pack off my back and removed the sturdy plastic storage bag inside. Cody fed the berries into the bag like they were precious little babies.

As he reached for more berries, a tiny sound

penetrated the jungle. I cocked my head, straining to hear what it was.

There . . . is that whimpering?

"Cody," I whispered. "Do you hear that? Sounds like someone crying."

Pausing with a bunch of berries in his hands, he blinked at me through glasses that had slipped down his nose. His mouth fell open, and he nodded.

Shit!

We scanned the area, then turned back to each other shaking our heads.

The jungle natives were the only humans for thousands of miles around, yet the mournful sobbing sounded like a woman. Maybe it was an animal or insect that I'd never heard before. That would make sense. In this rainforest, there were over one thousand different species of frog alone.

Cody and I exchanged a look of confusion.

I leaned into his ear and whispered, "Sounds like a woman crying."

"That's what I thought." He nodded.

"We need to find out and see if she's okay."

"Of course." He quickly cut away the last of the berries and secured them in my bag.

I swung the pack onto my back and connected the clips around my waist. Stepping over gnarled roots and dodging low-hanging vines, I led Cody toward the sound.

As the weeping grew louder, my mind raced with

confusion and worry. The tribal women were very private. Using Cody's interpretation skills, I had tried to communicate with them a few times. I was fascinated by how they survived out here in the middle of this primitive jungle and in particular, I was keen to learn what natural medicines they used. Some of the women willingly shared their way of life and seemed equally curious about me.

But the men made it known that they did not approve of my meddling or my interruption in the women's chores. Out here, the women had to breed, raise children, and do extremely onerous work, yet they didn't complain. They did what generations of women since the dawn of time had done. They didn't know any other way of life, and I had no intention of trying to change that.

Maybe oblivion is a blissful avenue to happiness.

I shoved through a bush with soft, wet leaves and stumbled upon Yamania, a tribal woman I had spoken to a few times, kneeling next to the lifeless body of a native man.

Yamania's face was etched with pain and anger, and her left eye was swollen and bruised.

"Yamania," I spoke softly, careful not to startle her.

Her gaze snapped to me, and her eyes narrowed, heavy with suspicion. The native man's body lay contorted on the ground. Vomit speckled his chin and the dead leaves on the ground in front of him.

Yamánia had tribal tattoos on her cheeks and chin. Green feathers were threaded through her ears and a thin stick was pierced through her nose. She wore nothing but a leather cloth around her waist and a necklace made of animal teeth.

"*Só quar!*" she shouted, her voice hoarse and angry.

"What did she say?" I asked Cody.

"Stay away."

"Please, Yamania." I stepped over a small bush toward her. "Tell her we just want to help."

Cody translated, walking forward a few paces. His fluency in the native language was impressive and his hand movements proved he was trying to calm her down.

She hissed at us and shuffled closer to the body. My breath caught. The man on the ground was Na-lynied, one of the tribal king's eight sons.

"Shit, Cody. That's Na-lynied," I said, aware that Yamania wouldn't understand what I said.

"Yes, I noticed." His fearful gaze swept toward me. *This isn't good.*

"Is he alive?" I studied Na-lynied's chest until finally, he took a shallow breath. "Oh, thank God, he is. Ask Yamania what happened."

"*Não é bem-vindo aqui,*" Cody asked.

"*Saia! Saia!*" Yamania screeched.

"She's demanding we leave them alone."

My breath hitched as I noticed a massive bunch of

Inocea berries next to Na-lynied's lifeless body. "Cody, look behind his back. What are they doing with all those berries?"

"Looks like he was picking them," Cody said.

"But why so much?" Frowning, I shook my head. It didn't make sense. Tribal people only picked and hunted what they could eat within two days. They didn't have refrigeration or sealed containers to keep food fresh. However, the quantity of berries Na-lynied had gathered was excessive.

I'd learned about the Inocea berry through the tribal women who told me they used the berries to heal wounds. They didn't eat the berry as it was bitter and full of unpalatable seeds.

For months and months, I'd had failed trials and tests. But two days ago, I recalled a comment that Arninadaal, Yamania's mother, had made several months ago: *The berry dies quickly.*

I had seen proof of how quickly the berry shriveled up. What I hadn't considered was if the medicinal properties in the berry rapidly diminished or even changed somehow once they were picked. It was a theory I was keen to test. Finding the berries and getting them back to the lab in time was the hard part.

"We need those berries, Cody."

He bulged his eyes at me. "We can't just grab them."

"Ask Yamania if we can take them."

Cody pushed his glasses up his nose as he translated my question.

"*Vá embora! Você não é bem-vindo aqui!*" Yamania's eyes flared as she screamed at us, her voice raw and enraged.

"Come on, Layla." Cody clutched my arm, pulling me away. "We need to go."

"What's she saying?"

"She says we have done enough."

"Done enough? What does that mean?"

Yamania shuffled behind Na-lynied's body, picked up something, and pegged it at us. A rectangular bottle landed in the mud at my feet.

"Son of a bitch." I picked up the tequila bottle.

"What the hell?" Cody's face contorted with confusion.

"Fucking Neville! I'm going to kill him." I undid my pack and slid the bottle inside next to the berries. "He must have bribed Na-lynied with alcohol in exchange for him hunting for the berries. No wonder we didn't find any in this area."

"Tell Yamania we didn't know. Tell her how angry I am at Neville." I spat my words, unable to contain my fury.

Cody desperately tried to convey my apology to Yamania.

She lunged sideways and picked up a stick. But it wasn't a stick; it was a spear. At the end of the spear was a dead monkey.

"Oh, Jesus." Cody covered his mouth with his hand, trying to mask the stench from the rotting animal.

Yamania yanked the spear from the monkey's carcass and jumped over Na-lynied's body.

"*Saia! Saia!*" She lunged at us.

CHAPTER 2

LAYLA

Yamania aimed the spear at us. "*Saia! Saia!*"

Cody and I put up our hands. "Tell her we're sorry."

Cody translated my words.

"Tell her we will punish Neville." I put my hands together, trying to convey how sorry I was.

We had no choice but to leave our precious berries.

I stomped away. "I can't believe Neville's fucking stupidity."

The dense foliage seemed to close in around me, making it even harder to breathe.

"I'm going to kill him. He's jeopardized everything." I stormed through the bushes with fury coursing through my veins.

As I led the way to my laboratory using the compass, the weight of betrayal sat heavy in my chest. Neville risked everything with his reckless actions.

"All those berries gone to waste." I clenched my fists so hard my chipped nails dug into my flesh.

Cody didn't say anything. He hated conflict. But this wasn't just conflict. Neville's actions could have killed Na-lynied.

"Damn him!" I said, but my words seemed to be swallowed by the oppressive humidity.

The sun didn't set for four more hours, yet I could barely see. As I pulled my headlamp from the side of my pack, my feet slipped out from under me, and crying out, I tumbled into a bush. "Goddammit."

"Layla. Are you okay?" Cody reached for me.

"Yes." Groaning like a wild boar, I wrestled myself free of the brittle shrub and grabbed his hand. "I'm just pissed off."

"I know. But you need to be careful."

"Don't you think I know that?" I slapped my hands, dusting off bark and leaves.

Cody jerked back.

"Sorry." I released a forceful huff. "I shouldn't take it out on you. I'm furious at Neville."

"As you should be. What are you going to do?"

I checked the mark on my compass and continued shoving through the bushes. "I'm going to give him a piece of my mind, that's what."

"Are you going to report him?"

I stepped over the giant log we'd straddled hours

ago. "I want to, believe me, but I can't risk his stupidity jeopardizing my research. I tell you what, though. He only gets one chance from me. Research or not, I will not risk the lives of these people or this jungle because of him."

"I agree. I hope he listens." Trepidation and worry laced his tone.

My fury hit a new level as I pictured Neville's smug expression and know-it-all attitude. "Oh, he will. Trust me."

A thought hit me like stinging nettle. Neville had been in this jungle two years longer than me. Had he been supplying the natives with alcohol all this time?

A wave of nausea washed through me.

Neville wasn't just a scientist. He was also the logistics specialist who provided essentials to the jungle lab: food, electricity, and equipment. He was in charge of the research facility and unfortunately, I needed him. But he also needed me. Prior to my tenure here, his research had stalled. It was ironic that we were both trying to create a skin ointment to treat burns. While my passion had been borne out of a tragic childhood accident, his had been purely financial, and he'd pitched his research idea to elevate his flagging career.

Initially, Neville had welcomed my arrival at the jungle lab. We'd pooled resources, shared hypotheses, and brainstormed ideas. I was very fortunate to have him, and I learned a lot from his extensive research on the plants in this region. But as the months went on, his attitude changed, and I believe he started to resent me.

I couldn't quite pinpoint the reason for Neville's change in attitude. Maybe it was because my research was progressing faster than his, or maybe it was because I was getting more recognition from my superiors at Blakely Pharmaceuticals than he was getting from his funding company.

Whatever the reason, it made working with him fucking horrible.

At the top of a hill, the laboratory came into view through the dense foliage. It was a rustic wooden building that was barely visible, but thankfully, the caramel-colored thatch roof stood out amongst the lush green surrounds.

Clenching my fists and mentally preparing my angry torrent at Neville, I stormed toward the lab which I was fortunate to have access to.

Over the decades, the eighties-built building had housed scientists, nature photographers, researchers, philanthropists, professors, students, National Geographic film crews . . . the list went on and on. Guests traveled from all over the world. Ten people could sleep in the building at any one time. It had two rooms with four bunk beds and one bedroom with two single beds. As there were only three of us here at the moment, we each had our own room. I wished I could say the same about the bathroom and toilet. Neville was a disgusting slob who didn't care who heard his bodily functions.

The bedrooms and my lab were the only rooms with four solid walls. Even the toilet and shower were outdoors. The rest of the building was screened with netting, which did an average job of keeping out the plague-proportion mosquitos and other bugs.

Aiming for the front door, I saw Neville through the netting. He stood next to the kitchen table and was eating something. *Obviously, his nausea was gone.* I unclipped my bag, removed the tequila bottle, and burst through the door.

"What the hell were you thinking, Neville?" I waggled the empty bottle.

Neville jumped back, spilling his food down his chest and onto the table. "Layla! Jesus?"

I threw the bottle at him. He ducked and the bottle slammed into a coffee mug, shattering both on the wooden floor. "You're bribing the natives with alcohol? You've jeopardized everything!"

"Jesus. Is that all?" Neville smirked. "We need those berries, and they know where to find them."

"Is that all!" I yelled, thumping my fist on the table, making his plate and cutlery jump.

"What does it matter how we get the berries?"

"Our projects aren't just about results, Neville. They are about ethics and sustainability too."

"Ethics?" Neville scoffed. "Ethics don't make

money, Layla. The world doesn't care how we get the berries as long as we deliver."

"I care!" My voice quivered with rage. "I'd rather have no ointment than a formula that threatens the lives of the natives."

"Threatens the lives?" He rolled his eyes to Cody like I was being a fucking lunatic.

"We just found Na-lynied lying in his own vomit." My hands shook with my rage.

"Na-lynied?" Neville feigned concern, but his eyes betrayed him. He didn't care about Na-lynied or his people. "He's young and strong. He'll be fine."

"He's not fine. Alcohol is poison to these natives. You could have killed him."

"Yeah, well, he's not dead, is he?" Neville flicked his hand like I was being irrational. "Did you get the berries off him?"

"No. He harvested a heap of berries, but he was too drunk to do anything with them. Because of you, those berries were wasted. You're a fucking idiot!"

"Hey! Remember who you're talking to." He aimed his finger at me.

"This ends now!" I yelled.

"Suit yourself. But without me you couldn't do your research in this fucking place, nor would you be as far along as you are."

I fought the rage crawling up my throat. "If you ever supply the villagers with alcohol again, I'll make sure everyone knows the truth about your ethics."

"Are you threatening me?" He stepped closer, towering over me.

"Yes. That's exactly what I'm doing." Holding my ground, I locked eyes with him.

I couldn't back down. Lives depended on me to stop Neville's stupidity.

I turned on my heel and stormed toward the hallway. "Come on, Cody. We have work to do."

I marched to the lab. As I strode to the counter that ran the length of the wall, I tried to force my brain away from Neville and Na-lynied and shift my thoughts into scientist mode.

"Jesus, Layla, that was intense." Cody's eyes were wild.

"Get the equipment ready," I said, ignoring his comment. "We need to work with the berries we found before they spoil."

As much as I hated to admit it, Neville was right. I needed him, and we needed those berries. Burns victims were depending on us . . . on me. I couldn't let my emotions cloud my judgment.

As I pulled the Inocea berries from the sealed plastic bag in my backpack, hope bloomed within me. Two days ago, I'd produced a successful formula that worked. But only once. My four subsequent trials failed.

It had been in the middle of the night when I'd recalled Arninadaal's comment that the berries began to die as soon as they were picked. All berries do to some degree. But these obviously deteriorated rapidly so we had to work fast.

As I set up my equipment, my excitement grew and the prospect of proving my theory was correct energized me.

Focus, Layla. Pushing aside the turmoil in my mind, I admired the plump berries. The bunches we'd picked contained about thirty vibrant, cherry-red colored berries with glossy skin and a smooth, almost perfect sphere. Studying them, I realized that the berries I used in my last batch had lost some of their shine, and shriveled enough to have softer edges and they definitely weren't as red as these.

Buoyed with this revelation, I washed my hands, pulled on my gloves, and grabbed my medicine tray from the refrigerated cabinet.

Behind me, the door hinge screeched, and I shot my gaze to Neville. "Get out."

"You forget who you are, Layla." He narrowed his eyes at me.

"Fuck you." I shuddered with fury.

He stepped closer. "Be careful or I'll have you booted from here and you'll never come back."

"Right back at you, asshole." Clamping my jaw, I glared at him until he pulled his gaze away.

I inhaled a calming breath. I couldn't waste any more time or energy on him. I directed my anger into measuring my dry ingredients and furiously grinding them into a fine powder in a mortar and pestle.

As Cody used a blow torch to scorch a specimen of pig skin that we'd sourced from the villagers that morning, I extracted the precious juice from the berries with a syringe.

"Let's hope this works," I muttered as I added the juice to the thick, fawn-colored paste. Working quickly, I stirred the elements together, then used a spatula to spread the ointment over the pig skin. Under a microscope, I studied the result with my breath trapped in my throat.

This could be the breakthrough I'd been waiting for. My heart raced with anticipation.

"Moment of truth," Cody said beside me.

"And?" Neville barked.

I stared at the specimen. The Inocea ointment shimmered, then turned a vibrant shade of purple. "It's working."

"It is?" Cody's questioning tone was full of hope.

"Look." I eased back for Cody to see through the microscope.

"It's producing froth," he said. "It's working."

"Are you sure?" Neville asked.

Cody stepped back for me to study the specimen again.

"Yes! It's a success." I exhaled, beaming with pride. "We have a formula that works."

I pulled back from the microscope, and Cody and I grinned madly at each other.

"I need to tell the board of directors," I said.

"Congratulations, Layla. You did it." Cody rested his hand on my shoulder and released a massive sigh as if the weight of the world was finally off his chest.

"Thanks, Cody. But it was both of us. *We* did it." My heart swelled with relief and joy. "Let's do another test. Prepare more skin."

Cody strode to the refrigerated cupboard.

"So, you really have a formula that works?" Neville's foul body odor wafted over me.

Reluctantly, I pushed back from the microscope. "Check for yourself."

As Neville peered into the microscope, Cody scorched the pig skin, filling the room with another foul odor.

"Huh. It looks like it's working," Neville said.

"That's because it *is* working. I had the formula right for months, but I didn't realize the berries needed to be freshly picked to work. That was the missing piece."

"Well done." His voice oozed insincerity and his smile made my skin crawl. But when his eyes sparkled, I shut up. I didn't need nor want his accolades.

Cody handed over the second piece of scorched flesh, and my hands trembled as I lathered the ointment onto the test sample. I positioned it beneath the microscope and peered through the lens. The tissue began to heal before my eyes.

"Amazing," I whispered, awestruck by the sight. A surge of optimism swept over me. The sacrifices, the long days, and the sleepless nights—they had all been worth it.

We've created a natural remedy that could change lives.

Neville vanished out the door, and I hoped he was getting us something to eat. At least that was something he was good at.

Working together, Cody and I tested sample after sample, timing our tests to twenty-minute intervals so we could accurately measure how long it took until the berries were no longer viable. We recorded our results with video footage of the ointment in action, and carefully documented the quantities and success. My stomach grumbled, and my brain just about hurt with the intensity of my focus.

It wasn't until we'd had four failed tests, which we documented on our timeline, that Neville returned to the lab carrying a tray with bowls of spicy pork stew and rice.

"Yum, I'm starving." Cody reached for a bowl and spoon.

"Thanks." I nodded at Neville, accepting a meal.

Neville stepped back. "So, when are you going to report this to Blakely?"

"As soon as I've eaten this and had a shower and

changed. I need to get these boots off." The rubber boots were great for outside in the mud but way too hot to wear much longer than that.

"Oh, so soon? You don't need to do more tests?" Neville's eternal negativity shone through his tone.

"No need. We have all the data we need. Right, Cody?"

"Absolutely." Cody beamed and his excitement was contagious.

"The stew was great, Neville. Thank you." I placed my bowl on the tray. "I need to use the bathroom, then I'll get my report on the go."

Leaving the lab, I walked down the hallway to my bedroom, unclipped my gun holster from my thigh, and stored both in the top drawer of my desk. I grabbed my clothes to change into and my mind was all over the place as I stepped out the back door into the darkness.

I pulled my headlamp up from my neck and turned it on. After I'd been in the air-conditioned lab, the humid air outside had my cotton shirt sticking to my skin. The generator was housed in its own insulated shed, yet its thumping metallic heartbeat still drowned out the jungle insects that would be a boisterous ruckus at this time of evening.

I placed my clothes in the shower cubicle, then gagged at the foul stench as I stepped into the outside toilet. The toilet was well overdue for emptying, but I was grateful that job was not mine. After checking for spiders or giant centipedes, I did my business and got the hell out of there.

When I'd first arrived at this jungle lab, showering in the open air had been a fun novelty. That quickly wore off. A hot shower was one of the few things I missed.

It surprised me how much I missed Hunter too. Our relationship never really got off the ground. We'd kissed a few times, freaking amazing kisses at that, and I had no idea why he made me feel like a randy cheerleader whenever he was near . . . but he did. I'd had a feeling he was gearing up to ask me on a date. If he had, I would have said yes. Until I got the go-ahead for this project, that is. Once that had been approved, I couldn't risk seeing him again. In addition to being brave and smoking hot, Hunter was smart, inquisitive, and protective. He would not have approved of my quest in the Amazon jungle. Which was why it was better not to tell him.

After I showered, I pulled on denim shorts and a long-sleeved t-shirt. I paused at the edge of the building to inhale the fresh jungle air.

An eerie feeling that someone was watching gnawed at my senses. I scanned the bushes but couldn't see anything. Unable to shake the sensation, I raced back inside with my heart pounding wildly in my chest.

I tossed my dirty clothes into a bag in my bedroom, made sure my feet were thoroughly dry, and pulled on socks and ankle-high hiking boots. As I returned to the lab, I tugged my wet hair into two long braids and secured them with bands.

Neville leaned over Cody who was writing something in his journal.

The acrid smell of burned skin permeated the air as my boots thumped across the wooden floor. When Neville jumped back, I squinted at him. *What's his problem?* Maybe my rage had scared him. Good. He hadn't seen that side of me before, but he was going to see a hell of a lot more now that I knew how low he would stoop to get his results.

At my laptop, I created a new email, addressing it to the four people on Blakely Pharmaceutical's board who had been monitoring my progress for eleven months.

As I began to type my email, a shadow loomed over me.

I glared over my shoulder and Neville's cold eyes drilled into me. A shiver raced down my spine.

God, I hated his creepy stares.

"Must feel good, huh, Layla?" His tone dripped with insincerity. "Blakely will be pleased."

"As will all the people who suffer every day with burns." I tried to keep my tone level despite my disgust. I couldn't let him see my unease. I wanted him to know I wasn't scared of him. If anything, he should be scared of me. The proof Cody and I had of his unethical practices in this pristine jungle would ruin him.

Neville stepped back.

"Let's celebrate tonight." A sickening grin spread across his lips. "I'll supply the food and drinks."

"No, thanks. I'd rather focus on finishing this report for Blakely."

"Suit yourself." He slinked back to the doorway, yet I felt him watching me.

My stomach churned with revulsion, but that only made me more determined to get this report done.

I will not let Neville destroy everything I've worked so hard for.

"Is the satellite phone charged up, Cody?" I asked. "We'll send this report as soon as it's done."

"Got it right—"

A blood-curdling scream ripped through the air.

CHAPTER 3

LAYLA

"Run!" Terror raced across Neville's face as he bolted toward the back door.

"What the hell?" I cried.

"Get down!" Cody dove behind a table.

My heart boomed in my chest as I scrambled in next to him.

Wild thundering noises echoing down the hallway sounded like bullocks stampeding through the building.

Screaming in anger, five native men stormed into the room. Na-lynied led them but I barely recognized him beneath his tribal war paint, and the fury blazing in his eyes.

Aiming his spear, he charged at Cody and me.

I screamed. "Please, don't hurt us!"

Na-lynied grabbed Cody's arm, and he cried out

as he was dragged to his feet. The terror in his eyes was loud and clear.

Na-lynied backhanded Cody's left cheek and Cody hit the floor without even using his hands to block his fall.

"Cody! Cody!" I scrambled toward my colleague.

My arm was yanked backward, and I screamed as I was dragged away from Cody.

"Let me go!" I tried to wriggle free from his grasp, but Na-lynied's fingers were a vice, digging into the flesh. One of Na-lynied's brothers grabbed me and pinned my arms behind my back.

A third native got in my face with his expression contorted into a snarl. "*Yagatara!*" he yelled so hard spittle landed on his chin.

"I don't understand." I shook my head. Without Cody, I had no hope of communicating with them.

Na-lynied tugged my arms harder behind me.

"Hey," I hissed.

Na-lynied slapped my cheek hard, and I stumbled sideways. My head hit the counter as I fell to the floor. Stars darted across my eyes as I fought the bitter edge between sanity and hell by pushing up from the floor. But my arms were weak, useless, and I slumped over.

"*Yagatara!*" Na-lynied's brother repeated, his voice a venomous hiss.

Glass shattered somewhere in the distance, and the men shouted and shrieked.

"Please," I whispered, clutching my stinging cheek and fighting tears. "I don't understand."

"*Yagatara!*" Na-lynied spat, inches from my face. His breath reeked of tequila and vomit, making my stomach churn.

I was dragged backward, and Na-lynied's older brother forced me onto the ground. He yanked my arms behind my back and as I cried out, tears stung my eyes.

"*Yagatara!*" One of the men shouted again as a rough vine was wrapped around my wrists, tying me to the metal leg of my desk.

Two men swiped everything off a section of the counter above me, knocking my precious equipment onto the wooden floor. As my research notes fluttered around me, a man hurled my microscope across the room. It slammed into the wall and broke into four pieces.

"Stop! Please," I yelled, but it only seemed to spur them on. They smashed test tubes and ripped papers to shreds, erasing months of research in mere minutes.

One of the men squatted inches from me. His face twisted into a dangerous leer.

Bracing myself for another blow, I shook my head. "Please."

"*Yagatara!*"

"I don't know. Please . . . I don't know what *yagatara* is." My chin trembled.

He slapped my face, and I fell sideways so hard my temple hit the floor. A piercing squeal rang in my ears and as they ransacked my lab, I realized this wasn't about revenge for what happened to Nalynied; this was a message.

We were outsiders, intruders in their sacred land.

We shouldn't be here stealing their precious berries and poisoning their warriors.

As they worked their way around the room destroying everything, a man figured out how to open the refrigerated cupboard.

He pulled out the bottles of alcohol and his eyes lit up. "*Yagatara.*"

I sat up and my jaw fell open.

"Is that what you want?" Desperation clawed at my throat. "Take it! Just don't hurt us anymore."

They laughed at my tears and began chugging Neville's alcohol, celebrating their find. They pulled items from the fridge, sniffed the contents, then smashed them on the floor. Nothing was spared.

The sickening scent of spilled chemicals mixed with the bitter tang of alcohol made me gag.

"Cody," I said softly. "Do you hear me?"

Cody was on his side, unmoving. His glasses were lopsided on his face and one of the lenses was cracked. Blood oozed from the cut on the bridge of his nose and had spilled over his closed eyelid. But he was breathing.

As the natives passed around the bottles, their wild laughter was like a knife cutting into my soul.

They've destroyed my priceless research.

This is Neville's fault. Where the hell is he?

A breath gushed from me. Was he dead? Did they kill him in revenge for what happened to Na-lynied?

As much as I loathed Neville and what he'd done, I would never wish that on him.

A native picked up my laptop.

"No!" I yelled. "No. No. No!"

His eyes swept to me with a mix of curiosity and malice. He bent the screen and the keypad open and closed like he was playing an accordion.

"Please. Don't." I shook my head. "I'll do anything."

A fresh wave of horror crashed through me as I realized that I hadn't had time to upload my research to the internet for a couple of days, especially today's successful trials. It was all on that computer.

I sat up. "Hey." I forced a smile and hating myself for this idea, I said, "You want more *yagatara?*"

He bent my laptop screen back until it wouldn't go any further.

Shit. Shit!

"*Yagatara!*" I yelled.

Na-lynied shot his gaze to me. His eyes conveyed both loathing and curiosity. It was as if he sensed the determination that burned within me to protect what mattered most to me—my research.

I nodded. "I have more *yagatara*."

Conflict raged in my mind between my loyalty and research for Blakely Pharmaceuticals, and my respect for the native culture. It was a war on my conscience, each side vying for domination.

Na-lynied pressed my computer harder, trying to force it open more.

"Hey," I yelled.

Neville had boxes of alcohol in his room. I'd seen him carry them in there. But never in my wildest imagination did I think he was sharing the alcohol with the natives. If I did, I would have tipped it all out.

Na-lynied looked at me with an expression that was so blank, I wondered if he was still drunk.

I shook my head. "No!"

He slammed the computer onto the counter, splintering the screen. He bashed the keyboard with his fist and when several letters dislodged, he jerked back, blinking as if he couldn't work out where the keys came from.

"Fuck!" I screamed, straining against the twine that bound me to the desk until the rough fibers bit into my skin. "Please. Stop."

A knot burned in my throat.

Na-lynied bashed the keyboard with his fist until all the keys became a jumble of letters and numbers on the floor.

I burst into tears. My proof of the successful

formula had disintegrated in seconds. Even worse than that . . . I couldn't come back from this. I would never be allowed back here. The villagers would never let me, or possibly anyone, do research here again.

Fucking Neville! This is his fault.

Oh shit! If he's dead, does that mean Cody and I are next?

As Na-lynied and his brothers continued to chug the alcohol from the bottles, I searched for a way to escape this nightmare. There were no windows and the only exit to this room was the door that led to the hallway connecting the bedrooms to the kitchen area. I would never get away before they caught me.

One of Na-lynied's brothers appeared in the doorway with a cardboard box in his hands. "*Yagatara!*"

He must have found Neville's stash of alcohol.

A couple of the others shouted, and when the man with the box strode toward the kitchen area, the others chased after him in a cacophony of drunken cheers that echoed through the destroyed lab.

"Cody. Cody! Wake up." I nudged his thigh with my shoe.

He didn't move.

I nudged him harder. Still nothing. "Shit."

I wrestled against my restraints until my wrists stung and my jaw ached from clamping my teeth so hard. Rubbing the twine up and down along the metal leg of the table, I chanted, "Come on. Come on."

It was no use. The rough twine was too supple to break.

All around me, the floor was covered in broken lab equipment. Using my foot, I shoved bits aside, searching for a shard of glass or anything sharp to cut the twine.

I gasped. The satellite phone was inches from my feet. Every muscle in my body strained as, inch by agonizing inch, I stretched across the floor. The twine dug into my wrists, but I ignored the pain, focusing only on the phone. Finally, the toes of my shoes gripped the antenna, and gritting my teeth, I pulled it toward me.

Lying on my side, with one eye on the door, I dragged the phone up to my face with my knees, and using my nose, I pressed and held the 'on' button.

"*Yagatara!*" One of the natives shouted again, making me jump. But they were too preoccupied with their drunken destruction to notice my small victory.

I stared at the screen as the phone came to life and a signal appeared in the corner.

Using my nose, I keyed in the only phone number I had ever memorized . . . Hunter Black, who I'd met when I did volunteer work at the burns unit in the military hospital. If anyone could help, it was him. He had access to equipment and friends who could rescue us from this mess.

"Please, Hunter, answer your phone."

His voicemail beeped.

Shit!

"Hunter, it's Layla." I kept my voice barely above a whisper. "I'm in danger. Please, send help. I'm at a top-secret research lab in the Amazon jungle. Access is only by boat. Coordinates are . . ."

Hoping they'd be enough, I rattled off the coordinate numbers I'd written on the whiteboard when I'd first set up this lab. I'd used them countless times during my research notes.

Shouts erupted down the hallway and panic surged through me.

"Please, hurry, Hunter." My heart jammed in my throat. "A native tribe attacked us but it's not their fault. I'm tied up. My friend is unconscious, and my boss has disappeared. Cody and I need help. But please, I don't want anybody killed because my—"

Na-lynied appeared in the doorway. His dark eyes filled with malice.

"Shit. Please, Hunter! Help!" I screamed.

Na-lynied charged at me and growling, he snatched the phone from my grasp. Confusion etched across his face as he jabbed the buttons with his stubby fingers.

I sat up, wrestling against the twine around my wrists.

"Please," I whispered, my voice hoarse and trembling. "Don't . . ."

Na-lynied leaned over me so he was inches away and as his face became a blur of rage and war paint, he said something I couldn't understand. But his tone sent chills down my spine.

He dropped the phone to the floor and his vacant black eyes flicked between me and my lifeline to the rest of the world.

"No! Don't!" Tears flooded my eyes.

He drove his spear through the delicate screen, shattering it to pieces.

CHAPTER 4

HUNTER

I STRODE AWAY FROM CONAN, my Belgian Shepherd, trying to mask my limp. But I couldn't. The burn scar across my right butt cheek pulled my skin so tight that the limp was there to stay, forever reminding me that I was damaged.

"Now I'll demonstrate an escalation of force," I announced to the crowd of eight potential clients. My voice was steady despite the unease gnawing at my gut. I loved working with the dogs and training them to be the best they could be, but it was a double-edged sword. The best dogs seemed to go to the worst assholes.

These people were civilians, not military personnel, and it was wrong to offer a dog like Conan to this bunch of pretentious bastards. But military dogs weren't in demand as much as they used to be. They'd been replaced with robots and drones. Dogs like Conan were now sought by bodyguards who couldn't do their job, and celebrities who wanted attention.

Sweat trickled down my back as I adjusted my thick padded suit, hating the weight and heat that came with the protective gear. I'd worn gear like this all the time in the navy. It never pissed me off like this back then. The thick gloves were cumbersome. The helmet's visor kept my face hidden and trapped my hot breath. The padding around my torso was bulky and annoying.

But all of it was necessary; Conan's jaw and teeth could crack through coconuts.

Fifty feet away, I turned back to Conan. He stood rigid and his eyes locked on me as he waited for my signal. He kept me focused, as did the sting from the burn scars that ruined me and my navy career. I raised my padded arm.

A murmur rippled through the spectators as their gaze flicked between me and Conan. I saw their curiosity but also their fear. Good. I knew what Conan was capable of, but they needed to see it for themselves. Conan was not a pet. He was a lethal weapon.

"Conan, attack!" I said, bracing myself for the impact.

Conan charged toward me, snarling and baring his teeth. My world slowed as adrenaline surged through my body. My heart raced as Conan leaped off the ground. His muscular frame crashed into me as his jaw locked around my raised arm. Unable to stay upright, I slammed onto the ground, but my training kicked in and I held myself rigid as Conan gnawed at my padding, trying to rip my arm off.

Conan's fierce growl was terrifying, and his attack was real, but also controlled. He didn't go for my neck and bite through my jugular. I'd trained him to go for my right arm, where most attackers would hold a weapon.

Conan snarled, snapping his teeth inches from my face. He was a terrifying sight.

The crowd gasped with their eyes glued to us.

"Conan, enough!" I said.

Conan released his grip on my arm and his vicious demeanor was replaced by a wagging tail. I patted him on the head, trying to catch my breath. The demonstration had gone well, probably too well. He would be sold today.

Conan stood two feet away, staring at me, ready for my next command.

I rolled onto my knees and tapped my thigh.

Conan came to my side and lowered his head.

"Good boy." As I patted Conan's head, he wagged his tail.

The crowd erupted in applause, and I allowed myself a small smile. I stood and with Conan at my side, I walked toward the crowd, fighting the limp in my right leg.

Does anyone notice?

Two years ago, I was a Navy SEAL, fighting for my country.

Now I was a damaged man, fighting to contain my anger.

I strode to the front of the crowd and instructed Conan to sit at my side.

"Any questions?" I scanned the faces of the potential clients and didn't like any one of them.

Jonas, in the front row, actually put up his hand. "Will he always be this aggressive?" He was so pale he looked like he was set to vomit.

He better not be serious about taking Conan. Jonas didn't have the balls for a trained dog like this.

"Conan will only attack on command." I kept my voice firm. "He's been trained to protect and serve, not to cause unnecessary harm."

The weight of their stares drilled into me. Judging me. *And* Conan, the dog I'd poured my heart and soul into training. I'd trained twelve Belgian Shepherds so far, Conan however was special. Yet just like the other dogs, he deserved a good home where his skills would be put to good use. I just hoped these people could see that too.

After no further questions, I patted Conan's shoulder.

"Conan." He stood to attention beside me. "Ready, boy?"

His ears perked up. His eyes focused on me with

44

unwavering loyalty. I took a deep breath, convincing myself that this was just another training exercise, rather than potentially Conan's last session with me.

"Observe the precision in which Conan follows my commands." My gaze swept to Tiffany McCann in the crowd. The famous movie star had caught my attention when I'd first introduced myself because her eyes were a similar color to Layla's. But that was where the similarity ended. Layla was a natural beauty who didn't need makeup or false laughter. Tiffany was the opposite.

I wanted to punch myself. Layla had made it damn clear that she wanted nothing to do with me and I hated that my stupid brain wouldn't forget her.

Slapping images of Layla from my mind, I showed the group Conan's remarkable obedience with a couple more demonstrations, concluding with him at my side.

"Good boy." As I patted his head, Tiffany clapped her hands and her cat-like eyes gleamed with excitement.

She was considering acquiring a dog for protection, but there was something about her that made me uneasy. Maybe it was the way her false smile never quite reached her eyes, or how her laughter seemed forced like she was trying too hard to be charming. If it wasn't for Tiffany's bodyguard who towered behind her with his arms crossed over his chest and his fierce eyes locked on Conan, I wouldn't even consider her as a prospective buyer for Conan. At least the bodyguard looked like he could handle a highly trained canine.

I gave Conan a pat on his rump. "Conan. Home."

Conan darted away, vanished through the door to his kennel, and pulled a rope to shut his own door.

The crowd clapped.

"Thank you for your time," I said.

They stood and most of them left without a word, confirming that I'd proven that Conan was not the type of dog they were after.

The scars on my back stung as I twisted out of the padded clothing, and my chest tightened as my stupid thoughts drifted to Layla again. Without her, I doubted I would have survived the pain from my burns. She'd been my lifeline . . . my sanity. She'd given me something to look forward to every day when all I'd wanted to do was punch out.

But she'd left without a word. That was what hurt. I'd thought we had something. I still couldn't believe how wrong I had been.

"Bravo! What a remarkable display of obedience." Tiffany's voice dripped with insincerity. I clenched my jaw, trying to hide my fury that she was still here . . . still interested in a dog that was way too good for her.

"Thank you, Ms. McCann." Forcing a smile, I had to remind myself that training dogs to sell was my job. I couldn't keep them all. "Conan is one of the best I have ever trained. His trust and loyalty is unquestionable."

I undid the Velcro straps on my protective gear and welcomed the cool breeze on my arms as I dropped the padded clothing to the grass.

"Indeed." Tiffany's gaze flicked up and down my body before settling on my face. "I'm sure that's not the only thing he's learned from you, Mr. Black."

What does that mean?

Is she flirting with me?

I fucking hoped not.

Shoving down the unease creeping through my veins, I forced my legs to walk toward her and Bruce. They were, after all, the only potential buyers left after the demonstration.

Tiffany sauntered toward me, swinging her hips like she was half dancing. Bruce trailed behind her with a look of disgust that told me he was not impressed with his employer.

"Can we discuss the details of acquiring Conan?" She leaned in close, and her perfume assaulted my brain.

"Ms. McCann, Conan is not just a pet," I warned, my voice tight. "He's a highly trained protector."

Her plump, glossy lips seemed to strain as she smiled. "That's exactly why we must have him."

"Are you sure you're ready for that kind of responsibility?"

"Of course, darling." Her fakeness grated against my nerves. "Money is no object."

"It's not about the money, Ms. McCann. It's about ensuring Conan goes to a home that respects his skills."

"Please, call me Tiffany." She batted enormous fake eyelashes that looked fucking ridiculous.

"Fine, Tiffany," I relented. As visions of Conan with this woman filled me with an overwhelming sense of loss, my thoughts slammed to Layla again. She didn't hide behind a fake façade. She was real and sweet and genuine. And she left me with a betrayal that gnawed at my heart.

I'D SOLD dozens of working dogs. I had no idea why I struggled with letting go of Conan.

I leveled my gaze at her. "I need you to take good care of Conan."

"Oh." She burst into laughter like I'd said the funniest thing she'd ever heard and rested her hand on my arm.

A shiver of revulsion crawled up my spine, but I forced a smile, trying to comprehend what could be so fucking funny.

"It won't be me looking after Conan." She palmed her chest. "Gosh, no. I wouldn't be able to control such a beast. Bruce will be his master. Won't you, Bruce?"

"Yes, ma'am." Bruce's voice was steady and professional. I appreciated that. No nonsense, unlike his employer.

Relief swept through me as I nodded at Bruce. "In that case, let's discuss the transfer. My office is this way."

"I'll leave you two to it." Tiffany waved us off, and doing that weird walk, she strode toward the limousine parked beneath the shade of the oak tree.

As Bruce and I walked away discussing the details of Conan's transfer and the compulsory training Bruce would need to do, I was conflicted between a sense of betrayal to Conan, and relief that he was going to a man who seemed capable of working with a loyal canine partner.

But this was the life I'd created for myself. The life I knew in the navy was gone, replaced by this strange existence filled with scars, unending pain, and a feeling that something was truly missing from my life. Yet I had no fucking idea what that was.

After Bruce and I finished discussing Conan's changeover, he shook my hand. "I promise I'll give Conan the life he deserves."

Certain that he meant every word, I nodded. "Good. Contact me if you need anything."

I scheduled Bruce's training with Conan and discussed payment and registration papers. With that complete, by the time I shook Bruce's hand, I was confident Conan was going to a good owner.

When Bruce headed for the limo, I headed for my bathroom.

I needed to get out of these clothes and have a cold shower.

In the bathroom, I stared at my reflection in the mirror as the lights cast harsh shadows on my face, highlighting my turmoil.

Stripping out of my clothes, I turned my back to the mirror and peered at the scars that twisted over my shoulder like angry red snakes, down my back and hip, and ended in a mass of lumps and mangled flesh on my right butt cheek.

"Fucking mess," I muttered as I traced the jagged lumps with my fingertips. Pain was my constant, lurking beneath the surface, ready to strike without warning.

It was a persistent reminder of the explosion on the aircraft carrier, the day my life was yanked out beneath me. My BUD/S training was the most brutal yet rewarding time of my life. It showed me what my body and mind were capable of.

The emotional torment haunted me. My body betrayed me. My scars robbed me of my sense of purpose and the life I thought I would have forever.

I was no longer a Navy SEAL. No longer invincible. And it pissed me off.

Now, all I had were memories and these fucking scars.

"Get your shit together, Hunter." I gritted my teeth.

My pain would never disappear. I had to learn to live with it. And my fucking limp. That was the real kicker. Before that accident, I could run fifteen miles straight in soft sand and knee-high water with my pack on my back.

Now I had to battle against that scar on my ass, and every step and every movement reminded me of how much my body was broken.

My only saving grace was that my scars could be hidden by a t-shirt and shorts. People didn't stare at me in sympathy or curiosity when they couldn't see them.

Shoving aside the self-pity bullshit, I jumped into the cold shower and scrubbed off the anger and frustration that threatened to consume me.

Thank Christ I was now part of Team Eagle. Having the camaraderie of my fellow ex-SEALs and the adrenaline rush of our new missions kept me going.

Grabbing a cold beer from the fridge, I headed to the porch.

The sun was sinking into the horizon, spitting golden-red hues across the sky. My one-eyed rescue dog, Luna, bounded onto the porch so fast her feet skidded all over the smooth timber. She wagged her tail and looked at me with her big brown eye, begging me to invite her onto her chair.

"Up." I patted the cushion beside me, and she jumped up, spun around three times, and sat looking out across our backyard like she owned the place.

"Hey, girl." I ruffled the fur on her head. "Another day, another dollar, huh?"

Luna cocked her head to the side, her one eye focused on me as if she truly understood every word.

Our bond had grown strong since I'd rescued her from the asshole who'd abused her so much she'd lost her eye. Thanks to my older brother, Preston, who had arrested that asshole for animal cruelty, Luna's previous owner had learned just how cruel humans could be during his six months in jail.

"I sold Conan today." I took a swig of my beer, enjoying the crisp, cold taste as it washed away the bitter memories of earlier.

Luna rested her head on the back of my hand.

"I know. I liked Conan too. But he'll be doing the job he's trained for."

Unlike me. The job I'd trained for could only be performed by elite soldiers in peak physical form.

Luna released a noise like she understood how much I yearned for my career.

"What?" I said before taking another sip of my beer.

She licked my hand. Luna didn't judge me for my scars or limitations. To her, I was a hero.

My phone buzzed and I pulled it from my pocket,

but not recognizing the number on the screen, I tossed the phone onto the side table.

"It's probably one of the assholes from today wanting to make an offer on Conan. Too late." I patted Luna. "Right, girl? We don't have time for pussies who can't make decisions."

She curled into a ball and released a massive sigh.

I sighed, too, and finished my beer. Maybe this life I'd created post Navy SEAL wasn't so bad after all.

But if that was the case, why did I feel like there was a massive crater in my heart?

Out of the corner of my eye, the blinking message button on the phone wouldn't go away. Whoever it was from didn't share their number. I swiped to listen to the message.

"Hunter, it's Layla."

My heart wrenched and I jerked forward, pitching the empty beer bottle across the deck.

"I'm in danger. Please, send help. I'm at a top-secret research lab in the Amazon jungle. Access is only by boat. Coordinates are -3.5002945124432516, -68.84761878654693."

"Fuck!" I stormed inside, phone in hand, and pulled out a pen and paper from a drawer.

"Please, hurry, Hunter."

My heart jammed in my throat at the fear in her voice.

"A native tribe attacked us but it's not their fault.

I'm tied up. My friend is unconscious, and my boss has disappeared. Cody and I need help. But please, I don't want anybody killed because my—"

She paused and I checked the screen to see if that was the end. It wasn't.

I jammed the phone to my ear, desperate to hear her voice.

"Shit. Please, Hunter! Help!"

Layla's scream pierced my fucking heart.

Stomping feet thundered down the line like cannonballs. A screech burst from the phone. A man yelled at her in another language.

"Please," Layla begged. "Don't."

Her scream was cut off and the call went dead.

"Fuck!"

My hands trembled as I listened to the call again, jotting down notes and the coordinates. After a third time through, I ended the call and my mind was like a tornado, swirling out of control. "What the hell is she into?"

I slammed my fist onto the counter, and Luna yelped.

Layla's phone number hadn't shown up on my screen. I couldn't call her back.

As I jabbed my speed dial number for Booker, the coordinates I'd written on my notepad stared back at me like a death sentence. "What the fuck is she doing in the Amazon jungle?" *Maybe she's on a satellite phone.*

He answered on the second ring. "Booker here."

"Booker, it's Hunter." I rattled off the scarce details I had from Layla's message. "I need to lead a team to rescue Layla and Cody from the Amazon Jungle."

"Jesus, Hunter." Booker's tone matched mine in intensity. "What's she doing down there?"

"I don't know. But we have to move." I paced the room with Luna watching me with fear in her eye.

"I'll round up Wyatt and the others," Booker said, proving he understood my determination. "Be at Team Eagle HQ in an hour."

"Make it thirty minutes." My mind raced faster than my pulse as I hung up.

Layla didn't want me when she disappeared without a goodbye. But we had something. Her call proved she felt it too.

No matter how much she pissed me off, I had to save her.

CHAPTER 5

HUNTER

I SPRINTED to my bedroom and as I grabbed the bag that I always had packed, I rang my neighbor, Judy, asking her to look after Luna and feed the other dogs. She agreed without hesitation, and she didn't ask questions. My clipped tone probably told her I didn't have time to explain anyway.

Scooping Luna into my arms, I kissed the top of her head as I strode back through my home. "I'm going away for a while. Judy will look after you." I put Luna on her rug in front of the sofa with a treat. "I'll give you more of those when I get back."

I grabbed my truck keys and raced out the front door without bothering to lock it behind me.

Normally, the rumble of my RAM 1500 truck drowned out my thoughts. Not today. Not when Layla's life was in danger. Driving to Team Eagle's headquarters in Yellowstone was a reckless hurricane of rubber screeching on asphalt and questions racing through my mind that were impossible to answer.

I had no way to let Layla know I was coming.

Every second was a ticking bomb, driving me insane.

At HQ, I skidded to a stop, and stormed through the doors and into the command center. Captain Booker Hayes and Wyatt Bixby had beaten me there. Wyatt, a former Navy SEAL like me, was calm and collected, his eyes laser-focused as usual. Captain Booker Hayes, the leader of Team Eagle and another man who I trusted with my life, strode forward with his hand out.

"Don't worry, Hunter. We'll get her."

I shook his hand. "I fucking hope so. I can't believe where she is." Scowling, I strode to our high-tech setup.

"Layla gave me coordinates." I sat at a computer and pulled Google Maps onto the main screen.

"She gave you coordinates?" Wyatt said. "That's unusual."

"Yeah, that's what I thought." I punched in the numbers Layla had given and the screen zoomed in on a satellite image of dense jungle, a tiny red dot marking Layla's location. "Son of a bitch! She's in the middle of fucking nowhere!"

"State of Amazonas," Booker said, shaking his head. "No wonder she had coordinates. There's nothing but jungle for hundreds of miles."

"Layla said the only way in was by boat. Along here." I pointed at a brown river snaking through the green. "The Amazon River."

"I bet there are crocs in that river. And piranhas. Oh, and giant anacondas. Sounds like fun." Wyatt grinned. "Count me in."

I clapped his back. "Thanks, Wyatt. Who else is coming?"

Booker shook his head. "Just us three. Everyone else is on missions."

"Fuck!" I slammed my fist on the table.

"Keep your head on, Hunter." Booker glared at me.

"Going in by river will take too long to reach her." Fear churned inside me. "We need a chopper."

"I'll get Charlie Cooper onto finding us a bird." Booker tugged his phone from his pocket.

Charlie always knew a guy who could get hold of any aircraft we needed, and his reach seemed to span the entire planet.

Booker pointed at Wyatt. "Give Stone Jacobs a call and have our clearances into Columbia and Brazil sorted."

"Yes, sir," Wyatt said.

Booker met my gaze. "Get our comms organized. We'll need a sat phone in that region."

"Copy that." I marched to our equipment cupboard and as I pulled out our gear, my mind slammed to Layla. It had been over an hour since she left that message.

Why the fuck didn't I answer my phone? If anything happens to her . . .

"Right." Booker clapped his hands, dragging me from my mental shit storm. "Charlie will meet us in Bogota, and he has a chopper ready for us when we land in Brazil. Grab your gear and let's roll. We'll make the rest of our plans on our way to the airport. Hank has a jet ready to fly us to Columbia."

With Booker and Wyatt at my side, a flicker of hope crashed through my mounting anxiety.

We boarded a private jet and flew out of Yellowstone toward Bogota, Colombia. The flight was long and turbulent, giving me way too much time to stew over Layla, and what the fuck she could be doing in the middle of the Amazon. She sounded terrified and as I replayed her message over and over in my head, another layer of dread stacked in my mind. We were taking too long.

"Hey, Hunter." Wyatt kicked my boot. "You remember that crazy mission in Panama?"

He must need a distraction; Wyatt was not a fan of flying.

I forced a half-smile. "Yeah, man. That was insane."

"Maybe this mission will top that?" He wriggled his eyebrows.

"As long as Layla comes out alive, I'll take whatever is thrown at us."

"That's the plan. Hey, maybe we'll see a tarantula." Wyatt grinned.

"As long as it's not on me, I'm up for that," I said.

"Or an anaconda, those things get huge."

I chuckled. "I'd rather not see a snake. You can handle them if we do."

Wyatt's grin got bigger, and he tapped his rifle. "Deal."

I nodded. "As long as it's animals we're dealing with, we'll be fine."

After a short stop in Bogota, Columbia where we picked up Charlie, we took off again and finally touched down at Aeroporto Internacional de Tabatinga, a remote airfield in Brazil, near the Colombian border.

I stepped off the plane, and the heat and humidity hit me like a brick wall.

"Welcome to the Amazon." Charlie beamed, showing off his gold tooth. "Chopper's over there. She's all yours."

He pointed to a dull black bird in the distance which had paint missing and a few dings in the sides.

"Jesus. Are you sure that thing can fly?" I groaned.

"Fly's better than that pussy-ass jet you flew in on. Trust me." He grinned wider.

As we strode toward the chopper, I pointed at a strip of silver tape near the door. "Is that gaffer tape?"

"Ah, yeah, but don't worry about that. Just a small hole, that's all."

"A bullet hole, by chance?" I cocked my head at him.

"How'd you guess?" He slapped my back, grinning like he'd won a bet.

"As long as it does the job, we don't care what it looks like, do we, Hunter?" Booker eyeballed me.

"Nope. That's our only criteria."

"Good work, Charlie." Booker shook Charlie's hand. "We owe you, man."

"You bet your asses you do. These guys drive a hard bargain."

Booker winced.

"Don't worry. Hank sorted it for me." Charlie winked.

"Thank Christ for Hank," I said.

"I'll second that." Booker grabbed his bag. "Let's gear up and get moving."

At one time, the military-style chopper Charlie had arranged would have been a beast of a machine with sleek lines and an intimidating presence. The MH-6 Little Bird compact helicopter was designed for speed and agility and was perfect for taking us into the dense jungle terrain. But this one had seen some action. The outside was dinged up and had its share of scrapes, and the inside had been stripped of all luxuries like seats and was rugged as all hell.

"Chopper looks fine to me," Booker said as we loaded our equipment onto the chopper.

Booker was right. We didn't need luxury. We just needed transport.

"I know you think I'm a miracle worker," Charlie said, "but I didn't have a choice. You got lucky, that's all."

I groaned. "Lucky will be getting to Layla in time."

"We're onto it, Hunter. Keep your cool," Booker said.

I tossed my bag into the chopper. "We're taking too fucking long."

"Then let's get you boys on your way." Charlie pulled Booker aside for a conversation Wyatt and I couldn't hear.

Booker climbed into the pilot seat and as Wyatt and I jumped aboard, the roar of the engines drowned out all other sounds. Despite my gnawing worry, a familiar rush of adrenaline coursed through my veins. It felt good to be getting into the action again.

Wyatt sat across from me with his face set in a determined expression. He knew the stakes just as well as I did.

Charlie leaned in our open door. "Good luck, boys. Go get her."

"You not coming with us?" I scowled at him.

"No can do, buddy. Got my own shit going on."

He saluted us and crouching over, he stepped back as the whir of the rotors blew his hair into a frenzy.

"Fuck." I thumped my fists onto my thighs.

"We don't need him, anyway." Wyatt's upbeat tone was obliterated by the concern etched on his face.

Booker took us airborne and within three minutes of leaving the airport, we crossed over dense jungle that stretched as far as I could see. Every mile took forever. Every minute took too long.

Every thought of Layla made my chest ache, and I couldn't shake the fear that we were too late.

Fucking focus, Hunter. I repeated the mantra over and over.

We crossed terrain that was straight out of a nightmare.

"It's gonna be impossible to land in this jungle," Booker spoke through our comms. "You'll have to drop in via cable and extract the same way."

"Roger that," I said, and Wyatt and I nodded at each other.

"But it also means I can't land and wait for your call. It'll take three hours to reach the coordinates, so we'll need at least three hours to get back. We only have enough fuel to give you four hours on the ground. Don't miss your taxi home."

I checked my watch and set my time.

"Four hours," I muttered.

Wyatt thumped my shoulder. "We've got this."

"Hell, yes we do."

Wyatt winked. "You must really like this chick, huh."

"Yeah. Pity she didn't feel the same."

He did a double-take. "She called you, buddy. *You.* That's one hell of a sign that she does."

"Three minutes to drop zone," Booker said. "You'll be about two miles from target."

"Affirmative." I clipped the cable onto my tactical vest and Wyatt did the same.

Below us was a sea of green vegetation. Not a clear patch of ground anywhere.

"Welcome to the Amazon," I said.

"Yeah. Where the spiders are bigger than your head, and the pigmies will eat you for breakfast."

I glared at him.

"What?" He shrugged. "Just stating the facts."

"Not helpful, Wyatt."

"This is it. See you boys in a few hours," Booker said. "Keep up the comms."

"Roger that." Hanging onto the drop line, I jumped out of the chopper, and the jungle canopy rushed up to meet me. "This is gonna be fucked!"

When I slammed into a tree's canopy, leaves exploded around me, and branches snapped as I bounced my way to the mud below.

Wyatt's grunts and groans confirmed his landing was as rugged as mine. As I unclipped from my tether, Wyatt slapped into the wet ground twenty feet away.

"Well, that was fun," he said.

I marched toward him. "Is your knee okay?" His knee had been reduced to mush in that aircraft carrier incident that ruined our careers, and his limp was worse than mine.

"It's fine."

"You right to roll?"

"Does a bear shit in the woods?" Wyatt flashed a grin.

The oppressive heat and humidity smothered me. Sweat soaked through my clothes, and every breath was like inhaling steam.

"Which way?" Wyatt asked.

I studied my GPS. "Northwest." I pointed in the direction and peered into the endless expanse of greenery. "Let's move."

Unfortunately, moving was slow. Mud squelched up to our ankles, and every step required a branch to be shoved aside. I led the way, hacking through thick underbrush with my machete. Bird noises and sounds from other creatures filled the air, but I couldn't see anything but enormous plants.

"Remember that snake in the mess hall that time?" Wyatt said as we stepped over a large fallen log. "Bet he's got nothing on the ones out here."

"Yeah, well, I hope we don't find out."

"You and me both."

As Wyatt and I took turns hacking deeper into the jungle, the ground sloped steeply upward. The thick mud morphed into a rough surface that crumbled away with each step. Roots from the massive trees twisted across our path and were as slippery as all hell. The pungent smell of rotting vegetation and the faint, sweet tang of something else filled the air.

Spindly vines wrapped around my ankles and several nearly tipped me ass over as I shoved through them.

"Fuck me," Wyatt said.

I spun to him and followed his wide gaze. A massive yellow snake coiled on a branch I'd just ducked under.

"Christ. I missed it. Is that an anaconda?"

The snake's scales shimmered in the dim light as if they were made of pure silver.

"Ain't no way I'm getting swallowed by no giant snake." Wyatt scrambled beneath the branch like his ass was on fire. "No way. Nah huh. Not this little black duck."

I shuddered at the thought of that thing being wrapped around my body. "That'd be a fucked way to go, that's for sure. Let's move. And keep your eyes open."

"Me? You're the one who missed that thing." He bugged his eyes at me.

"Sorry about that. You want to lead?"

"Roger that."

With Wyatt leading, we picked our way through a

minefield of vines and as many stagnant pools as there were running streams.

A terrifying scream echoed through the trees.

"What the hell was that?" Wyatt ducked down.

I crouched too and clutching my weapon, I scanned the bushes. "That better not be your fucking pigmies!"

Movement high in the canopy caught my eye. "Up there." I pointed to a pair of monkeys swinging through the trees.

"Fucking hell. It's just monkeys." Wyatt stood, shaking his head.

Huffing a forceful breath, I stood too. "Thank Christ! I thought we were about to be headhunted."

"Me too." Wyatt holstered his weapon.

The two monkeys became about fifty, and they were so loud it was impossible to hear myself think.

I checked my watch. "Damn it. We've already taken an hour."

If Wyatt heard me, he didn't indicate.

I confirmed our heading on the GPS and pushed in front of Wyatt, taking the lead again.

The damp, oppressive heat of the jungle closed in around me and my heart raced with both forcing through the unforgiving jungle, and my dread over Layla being trapped in this fucking place.

"What did you say Layla was doing out here?" Wyatt must be reading my mind.

"I have no idea. When I last saw her, she was

volunteering at the burns unit in the military hospital."

"Oh . . . she's the nurse you talked about."

"She's not a nurse, but yeah that's her. Layla Snowden." *Eyes that stole my breath. Hands that soothed my wounds. Lips that took me to another world. Heart breaker. Layla.*

"And she's the one who . . ." His words trailed off.

"Yeah, pissed off without saying goodbye."

"Right," Wyatt said like all the pieces slotted together.

At the top of a rise, I pulled my binoculars from my kit and peered across millions of trees. "There. Eleven o'clock."

Nestled among the trees was a thatched roof.

"It's got to be it," I said.

The building was barely visible, and it was impossible to see around the back or far side.

"Thank Christ." Wyatt pulled his water bottle from his hip and took a swig. "I was beginning to think this was some kind of sick joke."

"Nope. Not a sick joke, and neither are those natives guarding the hut."

He peered through his binoculars.

"I count four," I said.

The natives wore a loin cloth, bits of leather strapping around their calf muscles and biceps, and a whole lot of red paint on their faces.

"I see them. Are they wearing war paint?"

"It's not *happy to see you* make-up, that's for sure." My blood boiled as I studied the natives who stood between me and Layla. I wanted to rip their fucking heads off, but Layla's request echoed in my mind . . . *Please, don't kill anyone.*

My mind raced as I tried to figure out how we could get past them without resorting to violence. But I had to. I would do anything for Layla.

"Damn it." Clamping my fists, I turned to Wyatt. "We can't kill these guys."

He slapped the gun in his thigh holster. "Ah, yes, we can."

"Layla doesn't want us to, so we need to figure out another way."

"Wow." He raised an eyebrow. "You must really love her."

I scowled. Was this love? Or just some twisted sense of loyalty?

"All right then, Romeo," he said. "What's the plan?"

"Got any blow darts on you?" I joked.

"Ha! Left mine at home, sorry."

"There's only four of them. And I don't see a gun on any of them. Do you?"

He peered through his binoculars. "I see knives, spears, and bows and arrows. It's the wild fucking west."

"So, we sneak up behind them and take them down in a choke hold or a punch to the throat. Easy."

69

Wyatt shrugged. "Sounds like a plan. And if that doesn't work . . . then I'll shoot 'em."

"Done." I gave a nod.

I scanned the perimeter of the hut for weaknesses or openings. "Once we've incapacitated them, we go in through the front door."

"Ballsy." Wyatt smirked. He lived for this shit.

Me too. I loved training the dogs, but I would switch it up for this any day. Provided it went to plan. "I got the lead. Watch your six. Let's roll."

"Roger that." He clapped my back.

With my senses on high alert, I shoved through the dense foliage. Every sound, every rustle of leaves, seemed ten times louder than it probably was. Taking a wide berth from the hut, I clawed through the bushes until I stumbled upon a dirt track. Imagining that Layla had used this track many times, I crouched over and picked up my speed.

Just before the undergrowth gave way to the narrow clearing around the hut, I paused behind a bush with leaves bigger than my torso. The natives were so silent, it was like they were working in stealth mode. There was no friendly banter or orders being barked. The four of them stood like sentries guarding the hut.

They were all looking in the opposite direction to us, toward where the river was . . . according to the GPS.

"I get the impression they're waiting for something," I said.

Wyatt nodded. "Yeah. I don't want to hang around to find out."

"Me neither. You have the ugly one and the short one. I'll take the two with their asses hanging out."

"Bummer, I wanted them."

I rolled my eyes. "Concentrate. Follow my lead and don't kill them unless you have to. And don't get dead."

He saluted me. "Yes, boss."

Shoving down the desperation clawing at my insides, I dashed out from the bushes and sprinted at the biggest bastard of the lot of them.

He spun around. His eyes bulged and a shout burst from his mouth as he raised the bow in his hands and reached for an arrow over his shoulder.

Charging at him, I pulled my flashlight from my clip and whacked it across his throat. He fell to his knees. As I ran at the next guy, Wyatt sprinted past me and took down another native in a full-body slam.

The next guy was as scrawny as all hell. I wrapped my arms around his neck, clutching him in a chokehold. He clawed at my arm and as I held firm, Wyatt punched the ugly native's temple.

My man slumped in my arms. As I lowered him to the ground, my first guy screamed and raised a machete that was covered in blood.

Wyatt's other native pulled a knife too.

The crazy look in their eyes hit a whole new level as they charged at us with wild abandon. Wyatt and I stood our ground, fists raised, taking the attack full on.

I dodged the bloody machete and as my guy twisted his body with the blow, I kicked his knee. He staggered sideways, giving me a clear shot at his head. I punched his temple hard, and he crumpled to the ground unconscious.

Wyatt had his man on the ground, pinned face down with his hands behind his back.

"You got any cable ties?" He waggled his head.

As I looped the thin plastic over the man's fists, he thrashed against Wyatt's grip and screamed. The zip-tie did its work to secure him, and I slapped a piece of gaffer tape over his mouth to shut him up.

Wyatt limped back, dusting his hands. "Now that's how you do it."

"Yep." I surveyed the bodies around us. "These men aren't soldiers. They're fucking villagers."

Layla was right in her request that we don't kill them, and I was glad we didn't.

"So why the hell did they attack Layla?" Wyatt asked.

"Don't know, but let's go find out." With my heart still racing, I drew my gun.

The room beyond the door was screened with netting that looked like it had been shredded by an angry tiger, giving us a clear view of what was inside. The good news was that there were no more men in sight. The bad news was we couldn't see behind the door at the back.

I stepped over the broken front door and into a room that had a kitchen area on one side and an eating area on the other. The walls were lined with shelves housing strange objects, bones, and jars filled with unknown liquids. The room was dimly lit with a few candles scattered around and a strong smell of sweat, dirt, and something else that I couldn't quite identify tainted the air.

I gave Wyatt the signal that I was entering through the door, and he nodded.

A shout rang out behind us, and we ducked down.

Peering through my binoculars, I studied the area where the natives had been looking.

My blood drained. Men in tattered remnants of militia uniforms shoved through the bushes. Their eyes were cold and dead; their steps were slow yet with intent.

Every one of them held a rifle across their chest.

"Fuck," I said. "We've got company."

CHAPTER 6

LAYLA

THE OPEN DOORWAY provided enough dim light to allow me to see around my ransacked laboratory. The place where I'd dedicated nearly a year of my life was a shamble. My research—gone. My computer and satellite phone—smashed.

I still didn't know what Na-lynied and his brothers wanted. Why were we still alive?

And where the hell was Neville?

Cody groaned and his eyes flickered open.

"Hey, are you okay?" I asked.

It was a stupid question. He wasn't okay. A thick, red gash on his forehead had spilled blood down the side of his face, and the bruise around it was the color of a nasty storm. A lump had formed over his cheekbone and his swollen lip had a split through it that would be painful.

He'd rolled in and out of consciousness for a couple of hours and each time Cody had tried to communicate with the natives it had been like a game of roulette. They would either punch and kick him, or they'd give us food or water or let us go to the toilet.

He squinted at me, probably trying to focus without his glasses that Na-lynied had maliciously stomped on.

"Lay . . . Layla," Cody slurred, struggling to sit up. "Wha . . . what happened?"

"Shh, Cody," I whispered, my voice hoarse from lack of water.

Cody wrestled against the tattered twine tying him to the desk leg next to me as he dragged himself to a sitting position. "I'm so thirsty." Cody smacked his lips together.

"Yeah, me too."

"Hey!" Cody yelled.

"What are you doing?" I hissed.

"We need water. Hey!"

"Cody, shush. Please. They'll hit you again."

I couldn't stand to see him hurt any more. "Listen, we need to figure out what they want from us."

"What they want?" He squinted at me like I was just a shadow.

"Yeah. Why are they keeping us alive? Do you think Neville is . . . is . . ." I couldn't release the question from my throat.

"Dead?" Cody said. "I hope so. He deserves whatever happens to him."

"You don't mean that. He's an asshole, and I'll make sure he pays, but—"

"He's put our lives in danger. We're tied up and starving because of him."

"No, they want something from us. Otherwise, we'd be dead too."

Cody winced and his face twisted in obvious pain. He probably had a splitting headache.

"Maybe they want my research," I said.

"What for? They already use the berries for their own remedies."

"Hmmm. So, what could it be?"

"Human trafficking," he said deadpan.

"Don't be ridiculous." I glared at him. "Prior to yesterday, Na-lynied had never shown any brutality. That damned alcohol is to blame for what's going on here."

"So maybe they don't have a plan. Or maybe Neville is hiding in the bushes and they're using us as bait to get him back."

I nodded. "That could be an option. How long do you think he's been giving alcohol to the natives?"

"Years."

I gasped. "You can't be serious."

He shrugged and winced. The rough ties around his wrists left red welts that were so raw I could see them, even despite our poor visibility.

My research, the precious Amazon berries I'd harvested, and the ointment I'd hoped would change lives—it all seemed so insignificant now. The outcome of us being here had horrific consequences and now Cody and I were paying for it. "What have I done?"

"You haven't done anything wrong, Layla. This is on Neville. He was here long before us, and like I said, he's probably been doing this for years."

"Yes, but I was willing to take their berries and bring the outside world to their sacred—"

Shouts and cries of agony erupted down the hallway.

Heavy footsteps thundered toward us.

"Oh fuck, Cody. This is it! I'm sorry I dragged you into this."

A man filled the doorway.

He charged toward me and I screamed.

"Layla!" His eyes scanned my face.

"Hunter?" My heart leaped into my throat. "Oh my god! You came."

He sliced the twine binding my wrists and pulled me to my feet.

"Thank you," I whispered as tears streamed down my face. "I can't believe you're here."

"Yeah, well, we need to get the fuck outta here. You ready, Wyatt?" Hunter's frantic voice shot spears of dread through me.

The second man cut Cody free and helped him to stand. "Yep, let's roll."

Hunter grabbed my hand. "Layla, is there a back way out of here?"

"Yes. That way." I pointed down the hall. "What's going on?"

"Armed men are about to attack," Hunter said.

Wyatt supported Cody to stand.

"What armed men?" I asked.

"We don't have time to explain. Move!" Hunter pulled me toward the door.

"Follow me." My voice was surprisingly steady despite the fear crashing through me. I led them down the hall, past the dormitory room where the bunkbeds had been reduced to a pile of timber and a mountain of mattress stuffing. The windows had been smashed and it seemed every piece of clothing Cody owned was spread across the room.

My room had suffered the same fate, and my suitcase which had been under the bed was in two pieces.

Gunshots exploded somewhere behind us.

"Fucking move!" Hunter yelled.

I ran to the storage room which had also been trashed, and I climbed over a pile to get a clear view.

"There." I pointed across the room to the back door.

"Son of a bitch!" Hunter scrambled toward the door. Piles of boxes and gear were wedged up against it.

Hunter and Wyatt yanked the boxes away.

"Stand back." Hunter pulled his gun from his holster, shoved open the door, dove outside, and somersaulted into a crouch position, then panned his gun left then right. "Clear."

He waved us forward.

"Go. Go. Go." Wyatt shoved Cody and me out the door.

Hunter waved us to run past him into the lush foliage that seemed darker than ever. And sinister. Like even the trees had a death wish for us.

I reached the bushes first and turned to help Cody.

"Move!" Hunter hissed as he raced past me, running through the bushes like a bulldozer.

As we shoved through the vegetation, shouts and gunshots rang out behind us.

"What the hell is going on?" I asked.

"Layla!" Hunter urged me forward. "Just run!"

My heart boomed as we ran for our lives, charging deeper and deeper into the bushes.

Cody crashed into plants, and wet leaves slapped his face proving he couldn't see anything properly.

"Keep going!" Hunter paused and shoved us past him.

I grabbed Cody's hand. "I've got you. Come on." Squeezing his fingers in mine, I dragged him through bushes as big as elephants.

Brittle branches scratched my face and bare arms. My breaths were ragged gasps. My mind was bedlam.

I couldn't believe Hunter was here.

And I couldn't figure out who was trying to kill us. The natives didn't have weapons, at least not that I was aware of.

The jungle seemed to smother me, dragging my thoughts deeper and darker.

Cody stumbled and fell to his hands and knees.

"Shit, Cody. Are you okay?" I clutched his arm, helping him to stand.

"Don't stop!" Hunter caught up to us again, launched Cody to his feet, and dragged him forward.

The steep incline was brutal. Every step was forced.

"Where are we going?" My heart raced as I urged my body to keep up with Hunter.

Fat raindrops splattered onto our heads and the slippery ground became even worse.

"Keep moving." Hunter's eyes were locked on the GPS screen clutched in his hand.

"We've got company," Wyatt blurted.

"Get down!" Hunter's strong arm wrapped around me, shoving both me and Cody behind a massive tree trunk.

Cody and I screamed as bullets whizzed past.

Hunter used the tree for cover as he raised his rifle.

Panic bubbled inside me at the intensity in his expression.

He fired his gun.

A blood-curdling scream tore through the bushes.

Wyatt fired his weapon too. Hunter and Wyatt were controlled professionals. The men shooting at us fired wildly and their bullets ripped the plants around us to shreds.

Another man screamed. As did a third.

The hail of bullets stopped. Wyatt and Hunter peered down the hill through binoculars.

A silence fell over us that was as eerie as a funeral home.

Rain started again, slapping onto the leaves in a hollow, rhythmic sound.

My chest heaved with fear and exhaustion as I tried to catch my breath. My mind raced with thoughts of what might have happened if Hunter hadn't been there to save me.

"Are you okay?" Hunter's deep voice was tight with concern. His blue eyes, the color of an early dawn sky, pierced me.

I wanted to throw my arms around him and show him just how grateful I was that he was here saving us. "I'm fine," I choked out, forcing a brave smile. "Thank you."

"Let's keep moving." Wyatt glanced over his shoulder. "We've got a chopper to catch."

We continued up the steep terrain with Hunter

and Wyatt alternating turns at the rear of us, searching for the men chasing us.

The wild foliage seemed to close in on me, making it harder to breathe. Harder to walk.

Each time Hunter or Wyatt fired their weapon at the men chasing us, a scream followed. Men were dying and it was my fault. My narrow-minded quest to create something good brought this nightmare to the Amazon jungle.

And now three good men were in the line of fire because of me.

We finally reached the top of the hill and Hunter stopped us.

"Get down." He pressed Cody's shoulders until he flopped onto the wet leaves. I crawled in beside him and grabbed Cody's hand.

"Are you okay?" I asked.

He shook his head. "What's going on? Why are they shooting at us?"

"I don't know, but Hunter is here to save us."

Cody swept his wet hair from his face. "Who is he and how did he find us?"

"I met him in the military hospital I volunteered at, and I used the satellite phone to call him and gave him the coordinates."

As Wyatt peered through the scope on his rifle into the jungle around us, ready to kill, Cody moaned. His face was pale, and he looked dazed and disorientated.

"We're going to make it. I know we will." I squeezed his hand, trying to offer some comfort despite my own fear.

I looked up to meet Hunter's piercing gaze and saw not only the fierce determination of a soldier but also the vulnerability of a man who had been hurt before.

And it was my fault he was in danger again.

Hunter pulled out his satellite phone. "Eagle One, this is Black. We are ready for immediate extraction. But we are coming in hot. I repeat, we are ready for immediate extraction, and we have tangos in pursuit."

His voice was tense and urgent.

"Roger that." Hunter snapped the antenna down on the satellite phone. "Extraction confirmed. "We need to move."

We stumbled through thick underbrush, pushing toward an invisible location that only Hunter could see on his GPS.

"Keep going!" Wyatt yelled as he fired a few shots at our pursuers.

"We're almost there." Hunter pressed his hand to my lower back, urging me forward.

Our united breaths were ragged, and our bodies were slick with sweat and drizzling rain.

The distinct thump of helicopter blades cut through the air above.

"Get down!" Hunter pushed me into the bushes

along with Cody.

As we huddled together, Hunter peered through the scope on his rifle, his body tense and ready for action.

"Stay low," Hunter yelled over the roaring engine.

The helicopter hovered overhead but it was only just visible through the dense canopy. Wind from the rotors whipped my hair around my face and stung my eyes. The plants shuddered as if screaming their protest against this mechanical beast in their pristine wilderness.

"Here it comes!" Wyatt pointed to the cable lowering from the helicopter.

My heart raced. My hands trembled.

But Hunter was calm. Like this was something he did every day. Maybe he did.

"Let's do this fast." Hunter grabbed my wrist, pulling me to my feet. "You're first."

"What . . . me?" I stammered. "No, take Cody first."

"You're first." Hunter's gaze was intense and unwavering.

I had no choice. I swallowed hard. "Okay." I peered at Cody. "We'll be okay, Cody. It's nearly over."

I had no idea if he heard me or if he could even see me.

Hunter strapped me to a harness and attached the cable to a hook on his vest. His touch was firm and efficient, and each adjustment was made with precision and care. He tightened the straps, wedging my body against his.

"Ready?" His hot breath brushed my ear.

"Yes," I yelled over the thumping beat above us.

"Bring us up, Booker," Hunter yelled into his phone.

He gripped the cable, and I squealed as we were lifted into the air. Our bodies swung wildly as we ascended and I clutched onto him, burying my face in his chest, and tried to block out the terror racing through me. Branches and leaves whizzed by as we shot skyward, and it was an eternity before we reached the helicopter.

Hunter grabbed a rail and swung us onto the metal floor. "Grab on!"

I clutched a handle on the floor, and he unclipped the cable from his vest. It fell back toward the trees below.

He unhooked me from his harness. "You good?"

"Yes. I guess. Thank you." My voice choked with emotion and my body trembled.

His jaw clenched, and I thought he was going to yell at me. But he shook his head and leaned out of the helicopter to look down. The cable jolted and then shifted into reverse, pulling Cody and Wyatt up to the helicopter.

I shuffled back from the edge, ready to help Cody into the cabin with me.

A bullet slammed into the side of the helicopter.

"Oh, fuck. We're taking fire." Hunter aimed his weapon toward the trees and fired over and over.

"Cody!" I screamed.

"Get them up here," the pilot yelled.

The helicopter lurched and swayed. The sound of gunfire was deafening. Vibrations rattled us as bullets pelted the metal skin. Hunter yelled something, but I couldn't hear him over the noise.

"Get back," Hunter screamed in my ear, then he leaned right out the side and fired into the jungle below. Bullets whizzed past his head, but he didn't even flinch.

Cody and Wyatt appeared in the doorway, and I scrambled forward to help as Hunter pulled them in.

The front windshield exploded inward.

"We're hit. We're fucking hit," the pilot screamed.

"Get us out of here," Hunter said as Cody sat next to me, breathing hard.

Wyatt crawled into the cabin, then rolled onto his stomach, and leaned out the side so he could fire his weapon at the ground.

"Hang on," the pilot yelled. The helicopter shuddered as it dipped sideways.

A bullet punched through the cabin and slammed into the roof of the chopper.

Hunter clutched my arm and shoved me back. Fighting the scream in my throat, I clutched Cody's hand and gripped a handle.

The helicopter bucked and dropped like it had hit a massive air pocket. My stomach lurched as the chopper rolled to the side.

Cody screamed. Wyatt pulled himself inside and wedged his back against the wall of the cabin.

Hunter clutched the handle at the side of the open door.

"Come on, Booker, what are you doing?" Hunter yelled, yet he seemed so calm.

"Our hydraulics are gone." The pilot's knuckles were white as he wrestled with the gear stick.

The helicopter spun and dipped and lurched. Then it stilled, and I met Hunter's gaze. The fear in his eyes nearly crushed my heart.

As the engine roared, the pilot's face contorted as he struggled to keep the helicopter steady.

Out the open door, trees rushed past in a blur of green.

"Booker! What's the status?" Hunter shouted at the pilot.

"Trying to stabilize it!" Booker wrestled the gear stick, fighting for control.

The Amazon jungle whizzed below us in a haze of giant trees. Air whistled through the bullet holes and the smashed windscreen.

"I'm losing it," the pilot shouted over the noise. "Brace yourself. We're gonna crash!"

A scream tore from my throat as the helicopter tipped over and nosedived toward the jungle below.

CHAPTER 7

HUNTER

THE CHOPPER CAREENED out of control toward the enormous trees. I strangled the handle in my right hand and tried to reach Layla. She was too far away. Wind howled through the shattered windshield like a demon.

Layla's eyes were wild with fear. With one hand, she squeezed Cody's, and her other hand clutched a handle. Christ! She wasn't strapped in.

None of us were. It happened too fast.

"Booker, talk to me!" I shouted over the screeching engine.

"We're going down. Hold on!" His hands white-knuckled the controls.

"Layla!" I yelled over the chaos. "Get your seat belt!"

The helicopter clipped a massive tree in an explosion of leaves. Metal crumpled. Glass exploded. My team shouted, but the roaring engine and shrieking metal made it impossible to hear them.

"Hang on!" I tried to use my feet to hold Layla back.

The chopper hit hard, and the rotors sliced through the trees, shredding the blades to jagged bits of metal. Cody flew across the hold, smashed his head into the roof, and crumpled against the wall.

We jolted to a dead stop with the chopper nose down. Layla screamed as the jarring impact tossed her out the doorway.

I lunged for her. My fingers wrapped around her wrist. Her body dangled below the mangled wreck.

"Grab on!" I said.

Screaming, she swung her legs beneath her.

Fuck! We're still sixty feet in the air!

Her wrist slipped from my grasp. Her body twisted and jerked.

"Layla, reach up. Grab my hand."

"Hunter! Don't let me go!"

"Grab on!"

She tried to reach up. Our gazes locked. Her eyes blazed with fear.

Time seemed to still.

"Layla!"

Her hand slipped through my fingers.

"No!" My heart shattered as she fell away.

Screaming, she hurtled through the branches and

enormous leaves and thumped into the muddy ground.

"Layla!" I couldn't breathe.

My failure crushed me.

"Hunter!" Wyatt slapped my shoulder. "We gotta get this thing steady!"

I couldn't tear my eyes away from Layla's body, crumpled in the mud below. I'd failed her. I'd fucking failed her.

"Layla!" I screamed until my throat burned. "Can you hear me?"

Silence. My heart boomed against my ribcage.

She had to be okay. Had to be!

If I lost her! The thought was unbearable.

Layla . . . please be okay. I clenched my fist.

"Hunter!" Wyatt shook my arm. "Get your shit together."

I dragged my body back from the edge and fighting the ache threatening to consume me, I forced my brain to concentrate. The chopper groaned with my shift in weight and the metal creaked.

Wyatt pressed his fingers to Cody's neck. "Cody, you with me, man?"

Cody was slumped against the helicopter wall. Blood spewed from another cut on his head.

"He's alive," Wyatt said.

"Booker, you okay?" I shouted over the drone of

the dying engine. I shoved aside twisted metal to get to him.

Moaning, he tried to push himself back. His head had slammed into the shattered windshield and blood spilled down his face from a brutal gash near his temple.

We were lodged nose down, high up in a tree. Through the open cockpit, branches and leaves surrounded us like a cage, trapping us in a nightmare that we weren't going to get out of any time soon.

"I'm stuck." Booker's voice was barely audible above the chaos.

As Wyatt wrestled Cody's limp body into a seatbelt, I fought gravity to crawl toward Booker. "You're okay, buddy. I've got you."

The helicopter leaned at a dangerous angle, and I clutched onto anything to stop myself from slipping.

Booker shook his head. "My fucking feet are stuck."

My heartbeat drummed in my ears, drowning out the sound of the wind ripping through the shattered windshield.

"Stay calm." I clutched his shoulder. "We'll figure this out."

"Look at my legs," Booker said.

The cockpit had crumbled on impact, pinning his legs in the wreckage.

"Fuck, you sure know how to make a mess of yourself." I tried to make a joke.

"Tell me about it." He seemed more pissed off than in pain. Good.

"Is it your boots pinning you in place? Can you wriggle your feet out?"

He shook his head. "I've been trying. I'm gonna need to be cut out. And I don't mean my fucking legs." He glared at me like I was a maniac.

"I hear you, Booker." Panic rose in my chest. "Hey Wyatt, give me a hand."

"Hold your horses," Wyatt mumbled.

"We've got bigger problems than my legs." Booker pointed at the radio. The comms were a mangled wreck. "And the sat phone is gone."

"Fuck!" I fumbled with the damaged communications equipment, desperate to make the signal light come on.

It was dead. I flicked the switches. We didn't even have static.

"Son of a bitch!" I tossed the handset aside. The implications of dead radio equipment were huge. We were in the middle of fucking nowhere, with no way to call for help. *We're on our own!*

As I gritted my teeth, I tried to shove down my panic.

My thoughts were consumed by Layla. Her terrified face as she fell from my grasp was etched into my brain.

My duty to Team Eagle was my priority, but rescuing Layla tore at my insides.

"Hold on, buddy. We'll figure this out." I squeezed Booker's shoulder and eased back so Wyatt could view the situation for himself.

Wyatt leaned toward Booker. "Son of a bitch. That don't look good."

"It's fucked." The tone in Booker's reply clamped a fist around my chest.

Wyatt and I wasted too many minutes trying to free Booker's legs, but it was no use.

Holding onto a handle on the roof, I searched the helicopter for something to cut Booker free. "Damn it. There's nothing back here to cut you out, Booker."

I squatted beside Cody and tapped his cheek. He was still out cold. Picturing Layla's lifeless body, sixty feet below, made it nearly impossible to think straight.

"Go save Layla," Booker said. "I'll be fine."

"What? I'm not leaving you."

Gripping onto the roof, Wyatt wriggled into the back with me. He shook his head. Our situation was fucked.

The weight of choosing between them and Layla was a brick in my chest.

"I have to get Layla." I clamped my jaw, hoping Wyatt saw the distress crashing through me.

Wyatt nodded. "Go get her."

I hesitated, sweeping my gaze from Wyatt to Booker.

"Go!" Booker pinned me with eyes that were a mix of pain and determination. "We'll be fine."

Gripping onto the roof, Wyatt pressed his hand to my shoulder.

"Listen, we'll make it out of this mess." He sounded more confident than I felt. "Layla needs you. I'll look after Cody and Booker, and as long as those monkeys keep their distance, we'll be fine."

I huffed. It was just like Wyatt to make a joke in a fucked-up situation.

I swallowed hard. "When we don't return this chopper to Charlie, he'll contact Hank. Right?"

"Yep," Booker said.

"Then Hank will send a search party. Right?"

Booker nodded.

"That means the search party will go to the coordinates Layla gave us. Someone needs to get there to meet them and direct them back here."

"Looks like that someone is you," Wyatt said.

"Right. But I'll need to get Layla back up here so she's safe with you guys." Nodding my conviction, I leaned out the side of the chopper for the hook to the winch. "Ah, for fuck's sake! The winch is gone."

I peered down through the trees, searching for Layla. She still hadn't moved. I had to get down to her.

"We got any rope?" I asked.

Booker and Wyatt shook their heads. I searched the sparse chopper hold.

"Damn it." I tossed a mangled strip of metal aside.

"Looks like you're doing it monkey style." Wyatt shrugged.

"Agreed. But I doubt Layla and I will make it back up here."

Cody groaned, and Wyatt squatted at his side. "Hey, buddy. We've got ya."

He needed medical treatment. Layla did too.

"Right. I'll take Layla back to her lab with me. When the cavalry arrives, we'll bring them to you."

"See, I knew you'd figure it out." Wyatt winked at me.

I unclamped my jaw. "Yep. I'm coming back for you, so you guys hang in there."

"Very funny." Wyatt emitted a strained chuckle.

"You damn well better get your ass back here." Booker managed a weak smile.

"You have my word." I forced a grin, though my heart was strangled in a vice. "No matter what it takes."

Wyatt tapped my rifle. "No matter what it takes. Don't get a bullet in your ass."

"No way, Jose. I got enough scars to last me a lifetime."

I checked the contents of my vest and pulled out my GPS. Without that, I would never find this wreck in these trees. I programmed the distance between here and the lab.

"Shit. It's over twenty miles."

"You better get moving then," Booker said.

"How long do you reckon I have?" I asked.

"Charlie wouldn't worry about us for another six hours," Booker said. "It'll be too dark to send a search party himself. That's when he'll call Hank. Hank will pull a team together and they'll need to repeat our route into the jungle. All up, I reckon you have between sixteen and twenty hours. After that, you may miss them."

"I'll make it. Don't you worry. Make sure you have your flares handy. You guys got water? My bottle is nearly full. And I have four protein bars."

Both Wyatt and Booker had the same.

"We're good. Now get going or you'll miss our ride home." Wyatt met my gaze.

"Take care of yourself, brother." Booker managed a crooked grin.

"Always. Whatever you do . . . don't fall out of this chopper."

With a final nod at the pair of them, I swept my rifle over my shoulder and turned my attention to getting out of this death trap.

As I scrambled out of the wreckage and onto the massive branch that we'd crashed into, the weight of my decision to leave them nearly killed me.

But I forced myself to concentrate.

One wrong step and I'd be no fucking help to anyone.

CHAPTER 8

LAYLA

PAIN RIPPED through me as I blinked my eyes open. My body throbbed and stung, and my head pounded like it would rather explode. Sharp pains zipped across my back and legs. Above me, lush trees swayed in the breeze.

Where am I?

The jungle around me was dense and overwhelming, and the thick foliage seemed to press in on me from all sides. I tried to move but I was somehow stuck, and my muscles burned in protest.

"Help." I forced the word from my dry throat.

I pushed on the ground to sit up, and when my elbows plunged into thick mud, memories flashed across my mind. The helicopter. Falling from the sky. Hunter.

Hunter? Where is he?

"Hunter." My voice was barely a whisper.

Oh, Jesus. *Am I alone? Did he think I died in that fall?*

"Hunter! Help." My voice was swallowed by the oppressive vegetation around me.

Maybe he'd been forced away by those gunmen.

Oh God. Maybe . . . maybe he's dead. No. No. No. Please, don't let anything happen to Hunter. Or Cody or Wyatt.

A massive knot swelled in my throat.

Gritting my teeth to block the pain, I focused on the jungle sounds around me, straining to hear Hunter or Cody or the others.

The thick air was so humid, breathing was painful and my heart pounded like a drum. I tried to move and call out again, but my battered body refused to obey.

A sting pierced my arm and pain flared through me like wildfire. I gasped at the army of ants crawling over my skin.

"Shit. Shit."

Red welts covered my flesh like festering mosquito bites.

Jesus, how long have I been here?

"Get off!" I forced my uncooperative muscles to brush away the scurrying ants, smearing black mud over my stinging skin.

I have to get up before some other creature finds me.

Forcing myself from the muddy suction was like wrestling with a sloth. Every movement was painfully slow. My vision blurred, and dizziness threatened to overwhelm me. I sucked in huge breaths, fighting my swirling mind with clenched teeth and fierce anger.

Finally, I sat in the thick mud and as I summoned my energy to keep going, I scanned the bushes. "Where are you, Hunter?"

A distant growl echoed through the bushes.

What was that?

Fear twisted through me as I dragged myself out of the mud and crawled onto damp leaves. Every movement was brutal.

I forced my body to stand. My trembling legs were barely able to support my weight.

A creature hissed somewhere within the dense foliage. Swaying unsteadily, I scanned the bushes, searching for eyes staring back at me, but I saw nothing but vegetation.

I took a few shaky steps and leaned against a tree trunk for support. The bark was rough under my palms as I tried to steady my spinning head.

Breathe, Layla. And move. Breathe. Move.

The giant trees loomed. The silence hurt my ears and the dense jungle seemed to press in closer, suffocating me. I pictured jaguars stalking me in stealth mode. And venomous snakes coiled and ready to strike. And giant spiders and centipedes longer than my forearm.

And those armed men. *Are they still chasing me?*

I felt like my head was going to explode. Monkeys

screeched somewhere in the distant canopy. They were safe up there, high in the treetops. Down here, I was easy prey for any predator that crossed my path.

With a deep breath, I pushed away from the tree.

Don't stop. Don't give up. I can do this.

Tears burned my eyes and spilled down my cheek, and I flicked them away, angry that they were there. This was all my doing and crying wouldn't help.

Hunter must have thought I was dead. Why else would he have left me? Thorns scraped across my bare legs and snagged on my denim shorts as I put one foot in front of the other, forcing myself to move.

"Hunter!" I tried again, my voice strained and hoarse. "Can anyone hear me?"

Only the buzz of insects answered. Then, as if a plug had been pulled, they stopped. The whole lot of them. A crushing silence descended over me, so complete it swallowed me whole.

"Layla!" Hunter's voice pierced the jungle air, frantic and desperate.

"Hunter?" I spun to his voice, stumbled sideways, and collapsed into a bush.

"Layla! I'm coming."

Movement rustled high above, and Hunter emerged through the foliage, climbing down a tree. His face was etched with determination and concern.

My heart leaped at the sight of him.

He's alive--and he's coming to save me again.

Relief crashed over me.

"Hunter!" I tried to call to him, but my croaky voice was futile.

Blinking away tears, I rolled out of the bush I'd fallen into and slumped onto the damp ground. Dead leaves stuck to my muddy arms and legs, but I didn't have enough energy to pluck them off.

"I'm coming. Don't move." His frantic voice was laced with fear, yet his climbing movements were strong and controlled despite the brutal scars that crisscrossed his body.

"I'm here." I lifted a trembling hand, attempting to wave. "Here."

My feelings for him surged to the surface, filling the space in my heart I'd forgotten existed.

"Layla." The sound of my name, deep and raw, shattered my resolve and a sob burst from my lips. Hot tears spilled down my cheeks and I heaved so hard I couldn't breathe.

Hunter crashed through a bush. And there he was, bruised and bloodied, brave and beautiful.

"Oh, thank God." He rushed forward, his gaze devouring me like a starving man.

A messy lump of emotion sat in my chest as he pulled me into his arms.

As I hugged him, tears spilled from my eyes. He was real. Solid. Here.

"I thought I'd lost you," he murmured into my hair.

His words seeped into my soul. I squeezed my eyes shut, and sucking in air, I came alive, inhaling his scent.

He pulled back and relief flooded his face. "Layla . . ."

"Thank you."

His features were so perfect. Manly. Strong. His eyes told a story, and that story included me.

"I can't believe you survived that fall." He gave me one of his smiles that wrapped my world in a delightful bubble.

"I know. I think I hit every leaf on the way down and thank God for the mud." I showed him my mud-covered arms and pulled off a couple of leaves.

"You got lucky." A dozen emotions swept across his expression, and my heartbeat went crazy in my chest.

Frowning, I peered up at the helicopter wreck. "Where are the others?"

"They're still up there."

"Oh no. Are they . . . are they?" Words tangled in my throat.

"Cody was unconscious, and Booker's legs are trapped. Wyatt is good though, so he's staying with them."

Leaving those men cut Hunter to his core. I saw it in his beautiful, soulful eyes.

"So, what do we do now?"

He pulled the GPS from a pocket in his vest,

peered up at the wreck, and then pressed a button on the side of the device. "We go get help."

"How?"

"When we don't return in that chopper, our boss, Hank, will send a team to the coordinates you gave me to find us. So, we need to get back to your lab in time to meet them."

"But what about those men with the guns?"

He swiveled his rifle around to his chest. "Let me worry about them."

I nodded.

He brushed a strand of hair from my face. "Are you okay to walk?"

His tenderness was a delightful contrast to the rugged soldier figure he cast.

I nodded. "I can do this."

"Good." His crooked smile was weak although somehow also perfect.

My heart boomed in my ears, yet a calmness washed over me as he curled an arm around my waist to help me up and I groaned like my eighty-year-old grandfather used to. My head still boomed as if my brain was a jackhammer trying to force its way out of my cranium, and my legs were as weak as Jell-O. But I was alive. Hunter was right; my fall from that chopper was a miracle. Now we needed another miracle to save everyone else.

Hunter peered up to the mangled wreck. "I'm

coming back for you guys." Nodding at me, he reached for my hand. "Let's go."

I squeezed my palm to his, and although exhaustion was etched on his face, he dragged me forward with brute determination.

My legs were lead weights, and my lungs burned with each ragged breath.

Mud sucked at my boots, trying its hardest to pull off my shoes.

Hunter charged through every bush like an excavator and when he couldn't push plants aside, he trampled over the top of them. His boots stomped on twigs and squelched in mud. Each time we reached an obstacle, he cursed and yelled insults at the bushes. But I sensed the vegetation was not the only reason for his fury. It was probably me. With every minute, his anger seemed to increase and the distance between us did too.

A spiderweb wrapped around my neck and chin, and yelping, I jumped back.

"What's your problem?" He spun to me, and his fierce scowl scared me more than any giant spider could.

"A cobweb just—"

"What? Aren't you used to them?" He glared at me like I was evil, then turned and charged away.

Clawing at the sticky mess around my neck, I chased after him. "What do you mean?"

He karate-chopped a branch across our path,

splitting it into two pieces. "I mean . . . you're living in this fucking jungle, so you should be used to cobwebs."

"Actually, no. I'm not used to cobwebs. Nor will I ever be." I rubbed my hands over my head, making sure no spiders had migrated from that web to my hair. "No matter where I live."

If he heard me, he didn't show it. Following his GPS, he carved through anything that got in his way.

A bunch of matted creepers halted his trek. He grabbed a vine and yanked it hard, but when the vine won, he released a fierce growl and had to drop to his hands and knees to crawl beneath them.

"What's wrong with you?" I huffed.

On the other side of the living macrame, he hit me with a rage-filled glare. "What's wrong with me?" he yelled.

I darted my gaze to the bushes around us. If those men with guns were nearby, we were about to get shot at.

"You want to know what's wrong with me?" he said. Then, he shuddered like he'd had an exorcism and marched away.

I crawled beneath the vines, and the coarse ground scraped over the cuts and bruises on my legs. There was no need for him to answer the question. Everything was wrong.

He slapped a giant leaf, and a flock of birds darted out. He jumped then glared at the birds like they were poisonous darts. I half expected him to pull his gun and shoot the flock of Blue Dacnis midflight.

I cupped my hand over my mouth, trying not to grin at his obvious fright.

His gaze was a mixture of anger and confusion. "Why did you call me, Layla?"

I blinked at him. "Um . . ."

Because you're brave, and I knew you'd know what to do. Because your name was the first one that popped into my mind when I needed help.

I huffed. "Because your number was the only one I'd memorized."

He did a double-take. He hadn't expected that.

My gaze fell on an army of ants marching up a young Tangarana tree. "Shit! Fire ants." I pointed at thousands of venomous ants scurrying over the tree's pockmarked bark. "That tree and those ants can only exist with each other."

"Ah, for fuck's sake. The isn't a botany trip." He marched away.

Releasing a sigh, I chased after him. I didn't want to go into the complexity of my research project. Nor could I. I'd signed documents at Blakely Pharmaceuticals that swore me to secrecy. Then again, my contract was likely to be torn to shreds when details of this disaster were revealed anyway.

I wasn't wearing a watch, but the darkness quickly seeping into the vegetation confirmed we wouldn't have long before we wouldn't be able to see our own hands.

"How much further?" I called ahead to him.

"Twenty miles." He made a giant stride over a moss-covered log. "At least."

Twenty miles!

I squinted at the dense canopy about two hundred feet above and could just see red-hued fragments of the evening sky.

"What, Layla?" he said, shooting a glance over his shoulder at me.

I pressed my hands onto the log and straddled over it.

"Spit it out," he barked like I was one of his soldiers.

"What?" I dusted my hands on my legs and winced at a bruise on my thigh.

Hunter snapped a branch off a giant tree and speared it into a leaf on a *Coccoloba Gigantifolia tree* which was literally bigger than me.

"Hey," I yelled at him. "Stop wrecking the foliage."

He spun to me with his jaw ajar. "You're fucking kidding, right?"

"No, actually, I'm not. This jungle is pristine rain-forest, and it doesn't need men like you—"

"Men like me!" His eyes just about popped out of his head.

"Yeah. Men who have no respect for nature."

Releasing a fierce growl, he stormed ahead.

I trudged after him, trying to ignore the throbbing in my head, the burning ant bites and stinging scratches covering my arms, and the fury that Hunter exuded with every plant he shoved through.

The jungle was never-ending. The only constant was our footsteps and Hunter's grunts. I'd touched a nerve . . . yet I didn't blame him. He'd had to choose between me and his navy buddies. It was obvious who he would rather be with.

As the evening grew darker, the insects grew louder, letting their mating partners know that the sun was setting and it was time to get busy. Hunter and I were in for one hell of a night. And I wasn't looking forward to the moment when he figured that out.

How long had we been walking? An hour? Three hours? Out here, time lost all meaning. The jungle had night and day, and only two seasons, wet and dry. And even though we were technically in the dry season, it still rained nearly every day.

There were no paths through the jungle. Every step required us to step over something, through something, climb something, and when that didn't work, we had to go around something.

My foot slipped on a protruding root, and I tried to catch my fall by grabbing the trunk of a *Socratea Exorrhiza,* but the *walking* palm tree snapped off at the roots. Both me and the incredibly unique plant crashed into the bushes. I cried out as my face slapped into large wet leaves.

Stunned, I just lay there, catching my breath.

"Are you okay?" The concern in Hunter's voice surprised me.

"I'll live." I tried to lift myself off the ground, but I didn't have the energy.

"I know you'll live, Layla. I didn't ask that." He grabbed my hand and launched me to my feet. "Let's roll."

"Yes, sir." I saluted.

His foul glare made me regret that move.

"Sorry. That was uncalled for."

He rolled his eyes, yet I thought I saw a tiny smile curl along his lips before he marched away. As I followed him, my thoughts tumbled to the times we'd had together when I'd volunteered at the military hospital. He was the only patient I'd shared long walks in the gardens with. Yet despite his agony, he was the one who insisted we take the slow strolls. Maybe he wanted to escape the smells and constant sounds of agony from fellow patients in the ward.

During our lengthy walks, he'd pushed through his constant pain with tiny smiles like the one he'd just given me. But those smiles never reached his eyes. His injuries were brutal. Burn scars were some of the most painful wounds a human could endure. But Hunter was brave, a soldier in every sense of the word. Showing pain was considered a weakness. It damn well wasn't.

Somehow, we'd had a connection. Occasionally, his tiny smiles broke into laughter, and I would get a glimpse of the man he'd been before that fireball had ruined him. I so desperately wanted to help him get the old Hunter back, but that could never be. His scars were there to stay.

My ointment could help the next burns victim though, and the next. I was certain of it. That was why I needed to continue my research. I needed to tell my bosses at Blakely Pharmaceuticals what happened before they got wind of it and twisted the story around to it being my fault.

With renewed determination, I pushed through the thick underbrush, forcing my battered legs to catch up with Hunter. He was right; we had to keep moving.

A new sound added to the insects buzzing around my ears: rushing water. "The river is up ahead," I said.

"I know."

"Oh." I blinked at him, hoping he would elaborate on how he knew.

As the distant roar of rushing water grew louder, Hunter seemed to stride faster. The wet leaves we'd been walking on all day changed to jagged dark rocks that were both slippery and uneven, making the trek even harder. Hunter stumbled and when he grabbed a branch to save himself from falling, the branch snapped off, sending him sprawling onto a shrub with large dark red leaves that just about swallowed him.

"Son of a bitch," he shouted.

"You okay?"

"Of course I'm not fucking okay." He jerked his body out of the shrub.

"I meant are you okay to get yourself out of the bush. Clearly, you were." I swept my hand toward the non-existent path ahead of us. "After you."

He shoved an enormous palm frond aside and the leaf swung back to me, slapping my face. I stumbled sideways and sat, wedged between two giant, blade-like roots of a Kapok Tree.

He leaned on the massive buttress root and held his hand forward. "Give me your hand."

"Why are you so angry at me? Is it because I called you? Is that it? Well, you shouldn't have come."

"If I didn't, you'd probably be dead."

"You may be right. But at least I wouldn't have to listen to your grumpy ass bullshit."

"Yeah, well, this grumpy ass is trying to save *your* ass." He waggled his hand in front of me. "Now get up and get moving."

I slapped his hand away. "No."

He clenched his teeth so hard his jaw trembled. "Get up, Layla. We don't have time for bullshit."

"I'll tell you what we don't have time for, Mr. Navy SEAL. In about twenty minutes, we're going to be in pitch blackness. We're about to spend the night in the middle of the Amazon jungle, so we don't have time to hike anymore. We need to get ready for a night of hell."

"We'll walk in the fucking dark if we have to." He shoved his hand toward me again. "Get moving."

"No. I'm staying right here." I sat up and leaned back against the tree trunk which was wider than a bus. I couldn't have found a better place to spend the night if I'd tried. Nestled between the two giant roots was at least some form of shelter.

"Layla! For fuck's sake." He leaned further toward me. "Get up. Or I'll—"

"You'll what, Hunter?" I glared at him.

"I'll make you. If we miss the search party, we're fucked."

"You don't get it, do you? This is the Amazon jungle. Just about everything here is trying to kill you."

"Oh, I get it. Trust me. I've been in plenty of situations where things are trying to kill me. But what I don't get is what the fuck you're doing here?"

I blinked at him.

He glared at me.

"It's . . . it's top secret."

He burst out laughing. "Top secret! Oh, that's brilliant. Top *fucking* secret?"

"Yes. Top secret. I can't tell you."

"Fucking hell, Layla. This isn't a game."

"Believe me, I know it's not a game."

Groaning, he shoved off from the tree root and as he stomped away, he pulled the GPS from his vest. I expected him to stop but he didn't. He vanished into the bushes and kept on going. Pulling my knees to my chest, I brushed another bruise on the side of my leg and winced. I would hate to see how many bruises and scratches I had from that fall. And from Na-lynied's attack. That already felt like days ago.

A bird broke into song somewhere nearby, and its soulful tune was beautiful and captivating. Like she was singing for a long-lost mate. Maybe that was what I should do for Hunter, whistle or sing, so he could find his way back to me.

No need. He had his GPS. He would be back.

Which was why I was not chasing after him.

Holding onto the tree root, I lifted my butt and brushed away rough gravel and bits of bark beneath me. I sat again, but it was still as lumpy as all hell. Sighing, I stood and searched for Hunter, but the stubborn bastard had taken a hike. Literally.

As darkness descended, I shifted my search from Hunter to edible plants. I hadn't eaten since Na-lynied fed Cody and me scraps of dried meat that was probably monkey or wild pig this morning. The tree I'd been leaning against had some amazing medicinal properties, but unless we ended up with dysentery, it wasn't helpful.

I searched upward first, silently praying I'd see a

papaya tree or maybe grapefruit or oranges. No such luck.

Stomping boots and crushing twigs announced Hunter's return. Even his footsteps sounded angry. He charged through the bushes like a marauding bull. His clamped jaw and clenched fists demonstrated his anger had notched up a few levels in the time he'd been gone.

I had to bite back my instant thought to ask him if he was okay.

"What're you doing?" he asked.

"Looking for food."

"Don't worry about that. I found the river, come on." He grabbed my hand, giving me no choice but to go with him.

A light mist dampened the air. The ground became more slippery. The plants were slick with water and the slope changed, leading us down toward the river.

Hunter cried out and vanished before my eyes.

"Hunter!" I scrambled forward and came to a sharp stop.

As I stood at the edge of a precipice, Hunter crashed through bushes like a wrecking ball as he tumbled down a very steep slope.

CHAPTER 9

LAYLA

PANIC GRIPPED me as I peered over the edge where Hunter had fallen and searched through the bushes. I could just see him. He lay motionless at the bottom of the cliff, with his body splayed at an unnatural angle.

"Shit. Shit. Shit!" Hanging onto bushes, I sat on my ass and slid down the steep, unstable slope.

Rocks and dead leaves shifted beneath me. One wrong move and I could tumble down with him. My mind screamed at me to hurry, but taking a deep breath, I forced myself to keep my cool. Descending slowly and carefully, using tree roots and rocks as handholds, I shoved my bottom along the ground.

"Hunter. Please! Are you okay?" I could barely see him, but I saw enough to know he wasn't good.

My heart thundered in my chest, and the loose

rocks beneath me made every movement hell on my aching limbs.

Halfway down to him, the river came into view. The black water was flowing fast. Way too fast for us to swim across. It somehow glowed. Maybe the moon was giving it that light.

Each time I called to him, I hoped for movement, but he didn't give me anything.

Finally, panting and sweating, I reached him and knelt at his side. "Hey."

He groaned.

"Oh, thank God." I scooped his head into my lap.

"Wake up." I shook him and his body wobbled.

His skin was cold and clammy, and my heart clenched as my brave savior lay in my arms.

Moonlight bathed us in a silvery glow, allowing me to see the large lump on Hunter's forehead. Hopefully, it was his only injury.

"Jesus. You got lucky. The river is right there. You could have tumbled right over the edge."

Barely five feet away was a sheer drop to the raging water.

"Are you hurt?" I asked.

Hunter groaned. He had survived those crippling burns to his body. He'll recover from this in no time. But with him woozy like this, it was up to me to make sure we made it through the night.

I cupped his cheek. "Just rest, okay?"

The only reply was the buzzing insects in my ears

and the roar of the rushing river. All day we'd been surrounded by dense silence and oppressive heat. Whilst it was refreshing to be somewhat in the open, we were still in for a rough night.

I slipped Hunter off my lap, scooped loose rocks out from under his head and rested him down.

His eyes fluttered and he released a truly sorrowful moan. My heart broke to see him so groggy. But I'd seen him like this before, in hospital when he'd been loaded up with painkillers and fighting for his life. Seeing a man in his prime so broken was gut-wrenching.

"I'll get some things sorted, okay?" I touched his cheek, grateful to feel his warm flesh.

A small headlamp was around his neck.

"I'll just borrow this for a sec." I pulled the elastic strap over his head, flicked on the light and the beam was swarmed by moths and mosquitos within seconds.

Damn it. Tonight is going to be hell.

The mosquitos in this jungle could literally kill a human. I'd had every immunization possible to protect me from yellow fever, dengue, and malaria, and the mud covering my skin would provide some protection. Was Hunter immunized? In the navy, he would have been. But are his needles up to date? Fortunately for us, mosquitos liked stagnant water, so hopefully we wouldn't be bombarded.

My biggest worry was the other creatures: snakes,

spiders, killer frogs, and I hoped like hell a jaguar didn't come our way. I pulled Hunter's light onto my forehead and treading carefully, so I didn't slip off the edge, I searched for somewhere we could use as a shelter.

I found another Kapok tree and as I headed toward it, I picked up a stick in case I needed a weapon.

The buttress roots on this tree were taller than me, and the tree was one of the biggest I'd seen. It was probably about three hundred years old. I jabbed the stick between two of the enormous, exposed roots and pulled out the dead leaves that had accumulated in that space over time. Last thing I needed was to make our bed on top of an ant's nest, or worse a lancehead snake or some other killer that liked to hide amongst dead foliage.

With that done, I tossed palm fronds into the gap between the two buttress roots. As I worked, the sounds of the jungle came alive and I talked to Hunter as if he was awake, letting him know what I was doing, just so he knew I was there with him. It was a habit from my volunteer work at the hospital where sometimes it was impossible to tell if a patient could hear me or not. I would rather that than clinical silence which would make them feel so alone.

Adjusting the light so it didn't shine in his eyes, I knelt at his side and draped my hand over his arm.

He groaned and his eyes fluttered.

"Hey, there you are," I said.

His eyebrows bunched together, and he struggled to drag his eyes open. When he blinked at me, he seemed disorientated.

"It's me. Layla. You fell down a cliff and gave me one hell of a fright."

"Son of a bitch." He dabbed his head where an egg-shaped lump was forming and scowled.

"Take it easy."

Recognition flickered across his face. "Layla?"

"Yes. It's me. Are you okay?"

He cleared his throat. "I thought we agreed we weren't okay." His words were sluggish.

"Ha! There you go. Mr. Grumpy Ass is back."

Smacking his lips together, he sat up and swayed as he adjusted his rifle across his chest.

"Hold it steady there, mister. You had a bad knock to your head."

"No, we need to keep moving." Pain etched across his face as he leaned forward.

I pressed my hand to his shoulder. "Take it steady."

He scanned our surroundings and when his eyes focused on the water, I said, "Yeah, it's the river. You're lucky you didn't tumble right into it."

"Yep, but I didn't." He rolled onto his knees and after he stood, shook his head like he was trying to shift a fog in his brain.

"What are you doing?" I asked.

"We need to keep moving."

"Hunter . . ." I kept my voice steady despite my frustration. "Have you forgotten you just fell off a cliff and could've killed yourself?"

"Have you forgotten that we have a rendezvous that we cannot miss?" He took a wobbly step sideways and glared at me like he was warning me not to comment on his unsteadiness.

"Look," I said, "there's a difference between being determined and being determined at the detriment of your safety."

He leveled his eyes at me. "Says the woman who pissed off to one of the deadliest places on the planet."

"That's not fair." I shook my head and the headlamp beam crossed over his chest a few times.

He pulled his water bottle from his hip and drank. "It's not about being fair, Layla. It's about facts. And the fact is that if we miss that rescue chopper, then we're both fucked. As is your friend Cody and my mates, Wyatt and Booker."

I put my fists on my hips. "Well, here's another fact, mister. We can either take it slow tonight where we have no idea where we are going, and every step could literally plunge us into that croc-infested river. Or, come sunrise tomorrow, we can get moving and double our pace, plan where we step and where we're going, and possibly reach our destination faster."

By the time I finished, I was shouting like a maniac.

Groaning, he stepped toward the river and stood at the edge, staring into the tumbling water. He wore his anger in his rigid stance and stiff shoulders.

Fighting the urge to yell at him to answer me, I studied a Brazil nut tree which had to be at least five hundred years old because the fruit that contained the edible nuts was about one hundred and fifty feet in the air. The Amazon was like that, full of temptations. But the reality of harvesting those temptations were either impossible or brutal.

"I made a comfortable space for us," I said half-heartedly.

He scowled at me, yet his expression flickered with uncertainty. "We have plenty of light from that moon, and it will get brighter as it rises."

"No, Hunter. I'm not walking in the dark. It's too dangerous. Every step could be our last."

"Fine. You stay here. I'll come back for you."

Unsure whether he was serious, I decided to test his bluff and said, "Fine. Leave me."

He released another guttural groan. "Why do you have to be so stubborn?"

"Me! Pot, kettle, mister."

He turned his back to me to look across the river.

Hunter was six-foot-seven tall, sculptured in finely toned muscle. More muscle than when I'd looked after him in the hospital. I took a step closer, trying to bridge the gap between us. His trimmed beard covered a strong jawline, and his hair was a touch longer, allowing the slight wave to come through.

"Hunter, talk to me."

He peered at me over his shoulder, and the turmoil in his expression took my breath away. "Look, Layla. If you want me to beg you to keep moving, then here I am, begging. Please, can we keep walking?"

"It's not that I don't want to keep walking—it's dangerous."

"We'll walk along the riverbank where we can use the moonlight to see. And we'll take it easy."

"It's not just that. I'm so hungry, I can't think straight, and—"

He lifted a flap on his vest, removed a protein bar, and tossed it to me.

I caught it. "Huh. I should have known you'd be prepared."

"If I was prepared we wouldn't be in this mess."

"Hey . . . you couldn't have predicted that helicopter crash. Nobody could have."

"Eat." He nodded at the bar in my hands. "Then we'll move."

Peeling open the protein bar, I tried to keep my voice steady as I said, "I'm sorry, but I'm stiff and sore and every part of my body aches from that fall. I'm not an elite soldier like you. I can't keep up, and on top of all that, I'm tired."

"If there's one thing I know, it's that movement helps an aching body."

I swatted an invisible mosquito from my ear and sighed. He wasn't going to relent. Hoping I didn't regret this decision, I said, "Okay we'll keep walking. But only if you promise to go a bit slower. I can't keep up with you."

His eyes locked on mine, and in the moonlight, his stunning blue irises looked smokey gray. "That's a promise." His strong voice was barely audible over the rushing water and buzzing insects.

As I ate a bite of the protein bar, stewing over this decision, I removed his headlamp and handed it to him. In the filtered moonlight, a light sheen seemed to gloss his skin, giving him a heavenly glow. Hunter was a man in his prime, but his gloomy expression tore my heart out.

"I hope we don't regret this decision. Here, want half?" I handed the rest of the protein bar to him.

He waved it away. "You have it."

"You must be hungry."

"Hungry, yes, but not starving. I have three more protein bars. I'll have one when I really need it."

"Huh, did they teach you that in the navy, to push your body to the limit?"

"Something like that. Let's go. Watch your step." He pointed at a vine as big as my arm that crossed over the rock between us and disappeared over the cliff.

He offered his hand.

With half the protein bar eaten, I tucked the rest into my shorts pocket and took his hand. Our fingers intertwined, and it felt so natural like we'd been holding hands forever.

Hunter led the way, scanning the darkness around us. Insects buzzed in my ears and moths collided with my cheeks and eyes, adding to the disorientation of the night. The jungle was alive with sounds and smells, some fresh and special, some not so much. Every step crossed an obstacle of over-grown plants and slippery rocks, and the air was thick with moisture and humidity.

On our left-hand side, the river churned, and every once in a while, a splash hinted at the unknown dangers lurking beneath its surface.

Hunter grunted and jerked back, scraping his hands down his face. "Fucking spider web." As he peeled the sticky mess from his face, something rustled in the bushes beside us.

"Shit, what's that?" I whispered.

He shook his head and grabbed my hand. "Don't think about it."

"About what?" I muttered.

"About whatever that was. Just pretend you didn't hear it."

"They teach you that in the SEALs too?"

"Yep. Now stay close." The beam of his headlamp illuminated a white line into the vegetation around us, leading the way. Where the river carved a path through the jungle, the moon cast a faint glow over the water, bouncing enough light for me to make out shapes. Hunter moved with ease, despite his injuries, but I struggled to keep up.

Every step was a battle against the pain radiating from my bruises and scratches, souvenirs from the helicopter fall. But I couldn't let Hunter down. He'd risked his life to save me, and I needed to prove that I wasn't a pathetic woman who couldn't hold her own. I just had to keep moving.

"Watch out." Hunter held his arm across my chest. His headlamp shone on a yellow and brown snake coiled amongst the rotting leaves. Beneath its coiled body were the legs and fury tail of what looked like an Agouti. The large rodent wasn't moving; the poor thing had been crushed to death.

"Don't go near it, Hunter. The boa will only strike if it's protecting its meal."

"Want me to shoot it?" He wriggled his brows.

"What? No." I scowled at him until I realized he was joking.

Going around it meant either going deeper into the bush or closer to the river. He chose the river.

"Take it easy." He pointed at a shoe-boxed size rock in my way. "Watch your step."

Once around the snake, we moved away from the

edge of the water and continued through the seemingly endless expanse of darkness. The rocks beneath our feet were slippery and the moon cast as much light as it did shadows, making each step seem more treacherous than the last.

The weight of exhaustion bore down on me.

"Here, take my hand." He helped me over a felled log.

He paused to check his GPS and I swept my gaze across the trees around us.

"You good?" He tucked his GPS away.

"Yeah. I was just seeing if there were any edible plants."

He cocked his head at me. "Found any?"

"Not here."

"Okay, watch out for those roots." He reached out to steady me as I teetered over the mass of exposed plant roots. Hunter was all man, bound by muscles and brute strength, yet his gentle touch showed a different side to him. I forgot about the pain in my legs, the sting from my wounds, and the terror of our situation.

"Take it easy." Concern etched onto his features. "You're doing good, Layla." He squeezed my hand and let go.

"Thanks," I muttered, trying to focus on putting one foot in front of the other, rather than my feelings for Hunter that were growing by the minute. As we pressed on, his attentiveness to me never wavered.

He navigated the treacherous terrain with confidence, guiding me around sharp rocks, tangled vines, and slippery roots.

Hunter just kept going. And going. And my determination to continue became consumed by my exhaustion.

We reached a massive boulder that looked like it had tumbled down the steep cliff on our right hundreds of years ago.

Hunter groaned at the giant obstacle and shoved aside bushes to go around it.

"Hunter, wait. Please." My voice trembled with frustration as I leaned over my knees.

"You okay?"

"I just . . . let me catch my breath for a sec, okay?"

"Okay, take a few minutes. I'll check ahead." Yanking at the plants in his way, he stepped through the bushes and vanished.

The sounds of him crashing through the bushes were replaced by the ruckus of the insects around me. The rushing river added to the cacophony, and I leaned my back against the giant rock, and feeling the warmth from the day emanating from the stone, I inhaled a few deep breaths. I'd been in the jungle every day for eleven months, and yet I'd never felt as remote as I did right now. Before, my compass had always been my way back to safety. Without Hunter, I would die out here for sure. Many people had been lost in this jungle forever.

I was not going to be one of them.

My body throbbed and ached with equal measure. My thighs burned, and the bruises on my legs and arms were painful to touch. I had no idea how long we'd been walking or how much longer Hunter intended to continue before he stopped. I didn't know how much farther we had to go or if we would make it in time. Or if those gunmen were still at the lab, or if Neville was still alive. The never-ending questions were like ninja stars attacking my sanity.

Two days ago, I knew who I was, what I was doing, and what I wanted.

Now I couldn't answer any of those. My career would be down the toilet, the formula for my burn ointment was destroyed, and the idea of having to start over again was like a concrete block on my chest. I would need to find a new company to pitch my ointment concept to for financial backing. It took four years to reach the success I'd found a couple of days ago.

Now I was right back at the start.

A knot swelled in my throat.

My chest heaved but I sucked it back and clenched my fists. I had no idea if I *could* start over again.

Rustling bushes announced Hunter's return. "You okay?"

"Fine," I lied.

"Come on then. Time to roll." He held back a giant fern leaf for me to pass next to the rock.

Taking a deep breath, I pushed on, gripping the fern and forcing my legs to take me through the dense underbrush around the dump-truck-sized rock. My emotions were a hot mess by the time the river came back into view.

While Hunter charged ahead with the energy of a marathon runner, my legs threatened to buckle beneath me. My boot slipped and as I tumbled forward, my knee connected with a rock. Searing agony shot through my leg and a cry burst from my throat that was equal parts pain and frustration. "Shit!" Tears streamed down my cheeks as I clutched my leg above my knee.

"Hey. Hey." Hunter kneeled beside me. "You okay?"

"No, I'm not okay. I can't do this anymore. I'm not like you. I'm not an elite soldier. I can't keep up." The anger bubbling inside came out in my fierce tone.

"Okay, calm down."

"No, I won't calm down. This is stupid."

"Listen." His eyes locked on mine. "I know you're scared and in pain, but we can't stop. We need to keep moving if we want to be rescued."

"I can't go any farther." A sob burst from my lips, and I hated myself for it.

"It's okay." As he glided his hand over my back, he scanned the area.

The jungle loomed over us, darkness and thick vegetation pressing in from all sides.

"We'll rest for a bit. Come here." He helped me to my feet and pulled me into his strong embrace. His arms around me felt so natural and his warmth enveloped me like a protective cocoon. "You wait here, and I'll find a place for us to get comfortable for a few hours."

With his arm around my waist, we hobbled away from the river a couple of feet, and he lowered me to the damp ground.

His gentle touch had my anger morphing into bone-deep weariness.

"Stay here."

As he shuffled away, I wiped the hot tears from my eyes and nursed my throbbing knee. My body seemed to pound to one united beat, and I would hate to see how many bruises I would have come daylight.

The silvery moon reflected off the river, providing an eerie glow to the bushes around us. I closed my eyes, trying to block out the continuous drone of the bugs, and listened for Hunter's movements. He trudged back and forth somewhere in the bushes behind me, and I couldn't decide if his stomping was because he was angry at me, our situation, or the bushes that made every step an effort. It was probably all three.

As the giant fronds on a palm tree parted, Hunter returned.

"Righty ho, let's get you settled." He offered his hand.

Grimacing, I let him drag me to my feet.

"You know you're going to be more sore tomorrow," he said.

"Is that you trying to cheer me up?" I asked.

"Nope. Just stating the facts." Holding my hand, he led me through the bushes to the base of a rocky cliff where he'd layered a mound of palm fronds. He took off his headlamp and nestled it on the leaves so it shone upward. "Your bed, madam."

I chuckled. "Thanks. Did you check for spiders and snakes?"

"Yep."

"And frogs and giant centipedes?"

"Layla. Sit."

I allowed him to manhandle me onto the make-do bed, and the leaves crackled beneath me as I sat. "Ah, this is better."

He pulled a protein bar from his vest. "You should eat."

Leaning back, I pulled my half-eaten bar from my pocket and as I peeled back the wrapper, Hunter sat beside me, easing into my personal space. The warmth of his leg touched mine, giving me a sense of comfort.

I didn't shift away. I wanted him to touch me, and

not just fleetingly. Hunter was the only man I'd ever felt so comfortable with. He was interesting, and kind, and even when he was bursting with pain, he'd always asked how I was.

As I inhaled the earthy scent of the forest floor, I shivered at the damp chill that permeated the air.

"You cold?"

I nodded. "A little."

He sat back and parted his legs.

"Come here," he whispered, pulling me over so I sat between his legs. He wrapped his arms around me, draping me into his warmth.

"Thank you," I murmured, but my voice was barely audible over the chorus of nocturnal creatures.

"No worries," he said as he bit into his protein bar.

I shifted my position so I could see his face. "For this rest, and for saving me."

The light shone in his stunning blue eyes and as they met mine, the jungle around us seemed to fade away. Reaching up, I cupped his cheek, pulled him toward me, and pressed our lips together. Our kiss was somehow both delicate and desperate. He curled his hand around my neck, and my blood coursed through my veins as our kiss intensified. Every worry was stolen from my mind.

Hunter jerked back like he'd been bitten by an ant. "Layla." He sucked air through his teeth.

The way he said my name, like a painful warning, shattered around me.

He twisted me, so I faced away from him, and pulled my back to his chest. His arms draped over my shoulders, and he seemed to tremble as he held me to his body like just the touch of me hurt him to his core.

Unsure what to do, I placed my hands over his arms and said, "Sorry."

His head shook behind me. "No need."

He didn't elaborate, and a heavy silence fell over us that was soon replaced by the jungle and its buzzing inhabitants.

I licked my lips, tasting him all over again. Our kiss had been tender, yet also deep. We both felt something for each other. But once again, our timing was atrocious.

He cleared his throat. "Were you serious about giant centipedes?" He bit into his protein bar.

I huffed. He was obviously trying to shift his thoughts away from our kiss.

"Unfortunately. *Scolopendra Gigantea*, also known as the Amazonian giant centipede. It grows up to twelve inches and lives in moist, dark places like leaf litter."

"Right. Remind me again why you wanted to be here."

"For my research."

"Research into what?"

I sucked my lips into my mouth. When Hunter had been in hospital, he'd shared his emotions with me. To see a man fight pain, was to see a man broken to his core.

"That's right. It's top secret." Disappointment laced his tone.

I hated myself all over again.

And my heavy heart ached as much as my wounds.

CHAPTER 10

HUNTER

LAYLA'S KISS awakened nerves that had been burned to a crisp when my body became a fucking mess. My scars were hideous, and I was not the man I used to be. No woman would want me, especially a woman like Layla. She was too good for me.

But what hurt me more than anything was her inability to trust me. After everything we'd been through, she wouldn't share her research. *Top secret.* What a load of bullshit. Nothing was worth her risking her life.

"I'm sorry, Hunter." She seemed to crumble in my arms.

"Yeah. Forget it."

"No. I want to explain."

"You don't need to explain anything."

"I do," she said in a rush. "I signed contracts that force me to keep the details of my research a secret."

"Fine." I growled, pissed off that I was so angry over her reluctance to open up. "I don't care."

"I care, Hunter. I do. But you must know what it's like to have orders that require you to keep something confidential."

"Yes. Military secrets. But I knew what I'd signed up for. Did you know these secret contracts would put your life in jeopardy?"

"No, of course not."

"Then nothing could be worth this?"

"It's a burns ointment, okay?" she snapped.

"What's a burns ointment?"

She slumped even further in my arms. "I was working on a natural remedy to help heal burns victims."

"Christ, Layla. Is that all? You nearly died because—"

She lurched forward. "Is that all? Are you kidding? I saw what you went through. The pain! The scars! It's brutal."

"Believe me, I know." I shook my head, trying to force down those months of pure hell that I would rather forget.

"I'm doing this for you and my sist—" She stopped.

"Your sister? What happened to your sister?"

Pushing back from me, she shook her head wildly. "Nothing."

"Layla, talk to me. You can tell me anything."

The pain in her eyes nearly cut my fucking heart out.

"Did she die in a fire? Is that it?"

Her head slumped forward like she was looking at her navel. "No. No, she didn't die."

"It's okay. You don't have to tell me." I urged her to lean against me again. "Get some rest. We have a big day tomorrow."

She settled against me, but she was all rigid.

"Relax, Layla. This will all be over tomorrow. I promise."

Her shoulders softened against me. "Thanks for saving my life."

"I haven't saved you yet."

She cruised her hand along my arm, and it felt way better than it should. "You will."

"That's the plan," I said, trying to brush off the compliment. Truth was, saving Layla was more than just a mission to me now. It was my everything. My heart raced as I fought to focus on our surroundings rather than the woman in my arms and the lingering taste of her on my lips.

She deserved a man better than me. Someone who didn't have so much bullshit crashing through their mind.

"I'm sorry," she murmured, settling against me, her body was warm and comforting in the darkness.

"Go to sleep, Layla." I tightened my grip around her, and she seemed so frail in my arms. But she wasn't. Layla was brave. Any woman who came to the Amazon jungle to do research had some serious balls. This was no place for the weak.

I turned off my headlamp and pulled it back onto my neck so it was ready to use and blackness swallowed us again.

As my eyes adjusted to the moonlight filtering through the foliage, the jungle around me took on its own life. The trees towered above us like skyscrapers. The river bubbled and splashed over rocks. The damn bugs buzzed in my ears. I'd been in fucked-up places before where I had mud to my eyeballs and non-stop rain and insects that made me itch for weeks.

Somehow, out here with Layla, in her territory, it was also amazing.

As the smell of earth and decaying leaves filled my nostrils, my subconscious teased me with thoughts of us being together and having a life free from scars and secrets after this bullshit was over. Then I remembered who I was, and who she was and knew that was never going to happen.

Sleep came in fitful bursts, where I dreamed of Layla in my arms, and Booker trapped in the chopper and armed gunmen putting a bullet in my back.

The smell of smoke jerked me awake.

Fear clawed at my mind as I shook Layla. "Wake up."

Her eyes popped open. "What's wrong?" She sat up.

"Smoke. Can you smell it?" Standing, I adjusted my rifle and scoured the bushes.

"Do you see anything?" She dusted her hands on her bare legs.

"I see enough to know it's time to get moving. So, let's roll."

"Okay, just, um . . . give me a sec. I. . .." She indicated to the bushes.

"Roger that." I strode away, heading for the mammoth rock we'd had to dodge around last night. It seemed even bigger today. I took a moment to take a piss too. After I zipped up, I drank from my water bottle, and although the urge to wolf down another protein bar was huge, I forced the hunger pains twisting in my stomach to the back of my mind and peered into the bushes ahead.

"I'm ready." Layla stepped over a small shrub, showing off her long legs and her very sexy denim shorts. Hot damn.

Fucking focus, Hunter.

"Let's do this." I charged through a bush and a rugged vine wrapped around my neck, just about decapitating me. "Fucking hell. Great start to the day." I yanked the creeper from my neck and tried to tear it out completely, but the damn thing was stronger than me.

"You okay?" Layla asked.

"I'm peachy," I said.

Morning sunshine was coloring the sky orange and shoving the remnants of night away. "This way."

Continuing in the direction we'd traveled along yesterday, I kept the river on my left and the jungle on my right, gripped my rifle, and picked up my pace.

As the first rays of sunlight slanted through the dense foliage like laser beams, the smoke smell lingered, pitching my senses into high alert. Danger could be anywhere. Animals. Wildfire. Assholes with weapons trying to kill Layla for some damned burn treatment ointment.

Christ! What was she thinking, coming to this fucking place?

The question was pointless.

Time was against us. We had to reach her laboratory before the window for our rescue closed.

As we pressed on through the jungle, and Layla kept pace with me, my restless thoughts kept drifting back to that kiss. It was good. Damn good. Every time I looked at Layla, I wondered how different our relationship might've been if we'd met before that fireball ruined my life. But I had to face reality: I was scarred and broken, and no woman like her would ever truly want me.

"Hunter, look." She pointed to a bush covered in red and green berries. "It's a coffee plant. You can eat the cherries."

She tossed a few of the grape-sized fruits into her mouth.

"They're high in antioxidants which is why a lot of skincare companies use them. In fact, I include them in my burn ointment to—" She stopped. "Anyway, have some. They're better than nothing."

She forced a smile.

I plucked a handful off the tree and shoved them into my mouth. "Taste's okay."

"Yeah. Don't eat the raw bean inside though. It's not very—"

"Too late." I swallowed.

She giggled and it was the sweetest sound ever.

"Tell me earlier next time. So, what am I in for? Diarrhea? Vomiting?"

She laughed harder. "Don't be so dramatic. They just don't taste very nice raw. That's all."

"I can handle that." I shoved another handful into my mouth. "They taste a bit like watermelon."

"They do. The reddest ones are the sweetest." She delicately plucked a few.

"We don't have time for that." I slid my hand down the stem, dislodging about twenty into my hand. "Let's go."

I shoved one into my mouth, bit around the coffee beans inside, and spat them out.

As we continued our trek, I couldn't shake the feeling we were being watched. Every rustle in the underbrush made me want to shoot something.

It wasn't long before the humidity made my clothes stick to my skin, making me feel even more trapped in my own body.

Layla must have adapted to this heat because she kept up her pace, and every time I helped her over a log, or through a bush, her green eyes sparkled with determination, impressing the heck out of me. Most of the morning we hiked in silence, and I wondered if she was thinking about our kiss. I damn well was, and it pissed me off no end.

I pulled out my water bottle and offered her a drink.

"Thanks." She took one small sip and handed the bottle back.

I took a swig, hooked my bottle back onto my vest, and kept on going.

"So, Hunter," she said. "What have you been up to since you left the hospital?"

"Training military dogs mostly," I replied tersely, annoyed that she wouldn't open up, but expected me to.

Her eyes lit up. "Wow, that must be so rewarding."

"It sure is. I also do work with Team Eagle, helping out on private missions with Booker and Wyatt."

"What's Team Eagle?" There she went again, asking questions. But Team Eagle was something I was proud of. Especially the men I worked with. "My former Navy SEAL buddies who were also injured in that aircraft carrier explosion formed an organization that works for Hank and his Brotherhood Protectors. We operate a private airline, flying personnel around to transport weapons and equipment across the country and onto foreign soil."

"Oh wow, Hunter. I knew I'd called the right person when I rang you. So, is Team Eagle a military organization?"

"No, we take on missions the military can't or won't touch. Not quite black ops, but close."

"Sounds dangerous. Was I your first mission?"

"Nope. Last month we went to Puerto Rico to rescue Callie, a DEA agent."

"Did they save her?"

"Yeah. Wasn't all smooth sailing though, but we got her."

"Just like my mission, huh?"

"Yes to the mission going sideways, but no, we haven't rescued you yet."

"You will. I know you will. You really are a hero," she said softly.

I turned to her, and my damned heart skipped a beat at the admiration shining in her eyes.

"Hardly." I didn't like praise. Not when we'd lost men in the aircraft carrier explosion. That shit was fucked up.

Picking up my pace again, I marveled at Layla's resilience. As she matched strides with me, she pointed out animals and plants, even finding a bunch of bananas that were the sweetest I'd ever tasted. The sun rose high in the sky, casting dappled shadows on the jungle floor.

Layla moved gracefully through the dense foliage, her eyes scanning for any signs of danger or sustenance. I admired her toughness and cleverness but couldn't help but question her motives for being here. Something was off, but I couldn't figure out what.

My feelings for her grew stronger by the minute, yet I fought against them by focusing on the scars crisscrossing my body, a constant reminder of the ugliness beneath my sweat-soaked shirt.

"Are you okay?" Concern flickered in Layla's eyes.

"Fine," I grunted, unwilling to let her see the pain gnawing at my flesh.

"It's your scars, isn't it?" Her voice was tentative like that of a scared child.

Ignoring her question, I pressed forward.

"I can see you're in pain, Hunter."

I clamped my jaw, refusing to reveal my vulnerabilities when she wouldn't share hers.

"Hunter, I've seen your burns. I know what you went through."

"So there's no need to talk about them, is there?"

"Your pain is one of the reasons I'm out here."

"Bullshit, Layla." I spun to her, my patience wearing thin. "Don't put this on me. There's a lot more going on in that brilliant mind of yours than the fucking scars on my back."

She swept her gaze to the river, avoiding eye contact.

"If you tell me why you're in this hellhole, it may give me an idea of who the assholes are that we're up against."

"I don't know who they are. I promise." Her voice strained. "They have nothing to do with my research."

"How can you be so sure?"

"I just know. Trust me, it's not my research."

"Trust you?" I snapped. "Layla, you don't even trust me enough to tell me about your sister."

She clamped her teeth together hard and her jaw trembled. Her eyes flared with so many emotions I couldn't read any one of them.

"Forget it." I stomped away, and I couldn't give a shit whether or not she was behind me.

A short time later, I reached a section of the river-bank where the water was barely one foot lower than the land. The river was about eighty feet wide, and the distant shore was a blur of bushes.

I pulled out my GPS and frowned. "For fuck's sake!"

"What's wrong?" Layla wiped sweat off her forehead with her shirt.

"We have to cross the fucking river."

"What? Why?"

"Your fucking lab is that way." I pointed west.

She slapped her hand over her mouth. "Oh no. Are you serious?"

"Of course, I'm fucking serious." I turned to her. "I hope you can swim."

CHAPTER 11

LAYLA

"Are you nuts?" I swept my gaze to the Amazon River. "You can't swim across that."

"We have no choice. Can you swim?"

"It's not about swimming, Hunter. It's about the caimans, piranhas, and anacondas that live in that river."

He scowled at me. "Tell me you're joking."

"I'm deadly serious. We might make it across, but I, for one, am not risking being eaten by a croc or strangled by a snake."

"Son of a bitch!" He squeezed his head so hard it was a wonder his skull didn't crack.

This section of the river was wide and slow-moving, creating the perfect environment for the deadly animals to thrive. But narrow sections of the river were equally deadly because millions of gallons of water forced through its banks created rapids and waterfalls.

Pacing back and forward, Hunter studied his GPS again. "We're fucked, Layla."

"Is there any way to contact the rescue helicopter?"

"Nope."

"What about flares or something?"

"What about them?" If looks could kill, he just took off my head.

"Nothing. Sorry, I'm trying to be helpful."

"Yeah, well, you're not."

I sat on a boulder that was as big as a garbage can. Mud and dirt covered my skin in different levels of thickness, making me look like I had a nasty disease. The bruises covering my thighs were the color of storm clouds with an ugly yellow tinge around them, and the cuts down my shins looked like I'd wrested with razor wire.

Hunter strode to me, offering his water bottle.

"Thanks." I took a sip and handed it back.

"I still can't believe you survived that fall from the chopper." His gaze was on my legs.

"Me neither. I could have broken every bone in my body."

"I'm glad you didn't. It would have been a bitch carrying you all this way." A tiny smile crossed his lips.

"You think I'm that heavy, huh?" I grinned with him.

He shook his head. "Not heavy, just a pain in the ass. I knew you were trouble from the moment I laid eyes on you."

"Oh, really? Back in the hospital, you mean?"

He pulled me to my feet. "Yeah. Way back then."

My heart fluttered at the sparkle in his eyes. "I think you remember it wrong. You're the one who was trouble."

He gave my bottom a light smack. "Come on, troublemaker, get those long legs of yours moving."

"Troublemaker, huh? Where are we going?"

"I have no idea. I just hope we find a way across this river before it's too late."

As I set a pace in front of Hunter, I pictured him checking out my ass and my heart swelled like a balloon. I hadn't had many men in my life. I'd never had time for relationships, let alone love. I was married to my research and my volunteer work that enhanced my research. And when I wasn't doing either of those, I was catching up on sleep.

But there was something about Hunter that wanted me to change all that. For the first time in my adult life, I'd had a shift in priorities. I wasn't quite sure how he would fit into my life, but I wanted to make that happen. And that meant something else had to give.

As I led the way, our only constant was keeping

the water on our left. We reached a section where a huge landslide had dropped a massive chunk of land into the river creating a sheer cliff that we would have no hope of climbing.

"Shit." I peered up the steep face. "What do we do?"

Puffing out his cheeks, he swept his gaze from the rocky wall to the dirty water. "We have three choices. Go back and find a way around, climb up this giant divot, or swim around it."

"Okay, you pick."

He blinked at me, and I could practically see his mind churning. "We're going to make a swim for it."

I groaned. "I was worried you'd say that."

"We'll stick to the edge and move fast. At least the current is working in our favor."

I nodded.

"Good girl." He swept his rifle around to his back. "I'll go first. If you slip, I'll catch you."

"You better." I sat down to undo the laces on my shoes.

"What're you doing?"

"If I can help it, I'd rather not get my shoes and socks wet. It's no fun walking in wet boots."

"Your call," he said as he slotted the GPS and a few other items into a waterproof bag. "I'd rather my feet were protected in that river."

He had a point, but I decided to go with my plan. I removed my shoes and shoved my socks inside them.

Then I tied my laces together and draped my boots across my shoulders. Peering at the brown water, I sucked in a deep breath and let it out in a huff. "Oh, there's one other deadly creature I haven't told you about."

"Oh yeah?" He leveled his gaze at me. "What is it? Electric eel?"

I clicked my fingers. "Shit, I forgot about them too. But I was referring to the Candiru fish. It's only tiny, but it gets into places you don't want it to go. Whatever you do, don't pee while you're in the water."

His jaw dropped.

I burst out laughing. "You should see your face."

He cupped his groin. "Bloody hell, why didn't you do your research in Yellowstone National Park?" Growling, he shuffled to the edge of the river and slid into the water. "Let's get this over with. Give me your hand."

I sat on the edge of the riverbank and holding onto him, I slipped into the water up to my waist.

"Just stick with me. You can put your hands on my shoulders if you prefer."

"That's good. Thanks." My plan had been to hold onto his shoulders and swim behind him, but the current pressed my body against his like he was giving me a piggyback, and although he didn't say anything, he struggled to hang onto the shrubs and rocks along the riverbank.

"You okay?" I asked.

"Yep, except for the image of that damn fish swimming up my ass. Thanks for that visual."

"I didn't mean your ass. I meant—"

"Layla, I don't need the graphic details."

I chuckled. "Sorry."

"Ah, Jesus!" He jolted. "Something slithered between my fucking knees." He picked up his pace.

I slipped off his back on purpose.

"Layla," he called.

"I'm okay. Keep moving. I'm with you."

With bouncing strides off the muddy bottom, I let the current propel me forward. Each time my toes dug into the mud, slimy plants wrapped around my ankles and calves like tentacles.

The landslide seemed to go on forever. Whatever had been in its path when that section of land had tumbled into the river would have been obliterated. Surviving in the Amazon jungle was like that: part luck, part skill.

Hunter and I needed both.

Finally, we were able to pull ourselves from the water. Hunter climbed onto the riverbank first and plucked me from the river like I was a small child.

"See, that wasn't so bad," he said.

"No, actually, it was okay. Give me a sec to pull my shoes on." I sat on the rocks. "At least it washed all the mud off me."

Now that I could see my bruises and cuts better, my legs looked worse.

As he studied his GPS again, I let my feet air dry in the sun for a bit before I pulled on my socks and shoes.

He turned to me with a frown drilled across his forehead. "I smell smoke again. Do you?"

I sniffed. "Yeah."

He shoved his GPS away. "Let's go."

As we continued our trek, the scent of smoke grew stronger, and at a bend in the river, we had to crawl over the sun-bleached branches of a giant tree that had toppled toward the river a long time ago. As I straddled a branch thicker than my torso, someone shouted.

"Shit!" I tried to duck down, but it was impossible.

Standing on an enormous branch, Hunter clutched his rifle, sweeping his aim toward the dense bushes around us. Shaking his head, he waved me forward. As another shout drifted to us, we scrambled over the mammoth tree and hid behind a bush covered in purple flowers which was a species that I hadn't seen before.

Hunter pointed ahead, nodded at me, then clutching his rifle ready to shoot, he led the way through the bushes. I kept right on his tail and as the shouts became louder, the smoke dominated all other jungle scents.

Ducking behind bushes, we peered through the

thick greenery toward a small jetty and a derelict building on the edge of the water.

"Looks like an old church," Hunter whispered.

"It probably is." I kept my voice low. "For decades, missionaries have been using the river to find the jungle tribes who they try to convert to religion."

A boat appeared beyond the building, carving through the muddy water and as it neared the decrepit jetty, the sound of the motor cut through the silence.

"We need that boat." Hunter's stern expression matched the determination in his tone.

The boat's engine was turned off as it pulled up alongside the jetty. A man jumped off the boat onto the rickety timber and a rope was tossed to him from another man in the boat.

Hunter stiffened beside me. "They've got weapons. I need a better look. Let's get closer."

As we crawled through the underbrush, my heart pounded in my chest.

"Stay low." His voice was barely above a whisper. "And keep your eyes open. There could be more of them around.

Every sense was on high alert.

Crawling through the bushes was brutal on my battered legs, and adrenaline coursed through my veins.

Hunter raised his fist, and I stopped. I shuffled beside him and with our shoulders together, he peered through binoculars. Shaking his head, he handed them to me.

I adjusted the binoculars to see better, and my bones just about turned to Jell-O. "Oh, my god. That's Neville. I thought he was dead. That bastard is with those men."

Hunter grabbed the binoculars off me.

"He's the only Caucasian man amongst them."

"I see him." He lowered the binoculars to look at me. "Any idea what they're doing in that old church? Or this area?"

I took the binoculars off him and studied Neville. He had a rifle across his chest just like all the others did. I didn't recognize any of the other men. None of them were from any of the tribal villages that I'd been invited into since I'd been here.

"I don't know."

"Think, Layla. What's in this area that they would want?"

The shouts grew louder, and the scent of smoke hung heavy in the air. As my mind raced with thoughts of what the hell Neville was doing, smoke drifted over the rooftop of the old church.

"They must have a fire on the other side of the building," I said.

"Yes, I figured that," he said. "What would they need that for? What could they be burning?"

"What about coffee beans?" I blurted.

Hunter looked at me like I'd lost my mind.

"I'm serious. Those coffee cherries that we ate . . . they roast the beans that were inside to make coffee."

"Okay, I'll buy it. Why do they need weapons?"

Frowning, I peered through the bushes in time to see the men disappear inside the church.

"Maybe they have harvested other fruits. Like acai or Brazil nuts. Or they could be trapping exotic animals to sell. Or. . . oh, jeez. Maybe they're collecting my Inocea berry. Shit, Hunter."

"Hey, keep it calm." His eyes drilled into mine.

"I used the Inocea berry in my burn ointment. It was my unique ingredient and is only found in this section of the Amazon jungle. Neville had been bribing the villagers with alcohol in exchange for them to search for that berry."

"Now we're getting somewhere." He rolled his eyes at me.

My heart sank. "Sorry. I didn't think it was important."

As we hid behind the bush watching the old church, I told Hunter about Neville, who he was, and how he was working for another pharmaceutical company to create a burns ointment. How he'd been living here for four years, and how he'd initially helped me but then became a lazy bastard who gave alcohol to the natives. "He ruined everything," I said.

"Sounds like an asshole." Hunter snarled.

"He is. I thought he was dead. He must have

known that Cody and I had been captured, and he didn't try to help us."

Hunter moaned. "So do you want him dead or not?"

"What?" My jaw dropped.

"We need that boat, and I doubt they're going to let us take it from them easily. So, depending on how this plays out, some of those men are going to die today."

"Shit, Hunter, I don't know if I can live with that." I tried to keep my voice steady as my heart hammered in my chest.

Hunter peered through his binoculars again and his breath hitched. "Got a visual on another man. Looks like a mean motherfucker too."

He handed the binoculars to me.

My chest nearly caved in.

"Oh Jesus, it's Na-lynied. He's the youngest son of the Manouthiciara tribe's king. He shouldn't be here. He should be with his tribe, in the middle of the jungle, hunting and foraging for his family." I clenched my fist. "Neville has corrupted them all."

My muscles ached as a wave of utter uselessness washed through me. "We've brought this upon them. Those poor villagers."

Hunter clutched the back of my hand. "You didn't. That asshole did. So, my question still stands. Do you want me to kill him?"

"No, Hunter, I don't. He deserves to be punished for what he's done, but not . . . not that."

"I'm not making any promises. If I have to choose between saving you or killing him, it's a no-brainer for me. We can't waste any more time." He studied through the binoculars.

"What do we do?"

With each passing moment, the stakes grew higher, and the tension between Hunter and me threatened to consume me. We were about to plunge headfirst into danger and one thing was clear: our lives were on the line. Once we made our move, there would be no turning back.

He shifted his gaze to me. "Would you rather swim or shoot?"

"Depends on what I'm shooting at?"

He cocked his head and didn't need to say anything else.

"I'm not shooting anyone if that's what you mean."

The expression on his face morphed to deadly serious. "I need you to swim to that boat, unhook it, and drift downstream with it."

I blinked at him, waiting for the punch line. "Shit. You're serious, aren't you? What are you going to do?"

"I'm going to shoot anyone who tries to stop you."

CHAPTER 12

HUNTER

MY PLAN WAS NOT IDEAL. It wasn't even close to it, but it was all we had. Time was running out. We couldn't wait until dark, and we couldn't risk them getting back in that boat and pissing off with our only transport across this river. We had to act now. As much as I hated doing this, I needed Layla on board with me.

"Jesus." Layla's breath hitched. "I'm not sure—"

I shifted my position so I could look directly at her. "We have no choice. We need that boat, and either I go in there guns blazing and shoot the lot of them, or we try to steal the boat out from under them."

She rolled her head back, giving me a glorious view of her long neck.

"We need to act fast," I said, "before they take that boat."

She sucked her lips into her mouth, and the turmoil in her expression just about did me in.

I gripped the back of her hand. "You can do this. I know you can."

She huffed out a breath. "Tell me what to do."

"Good girl." As I handed the binoculars to her, I pointed to a rocky outcrop downstream. "See those rocks that stick out into the river? That's where I'll be. From that spot, I'll be able to see you, and them. I'll cover you, okay?"

She lowered the binoculars. "What do I do?"

My heart just about stopped at the fear in her eyes. This was a bad idea. I should just go into the old church and shoot the lot of them. "We can do this another way."

"Shoot everyone?" She shook her head.

"Yes, that. Or we can try to negotiate. But what do we have to bargain with?"

Her shoulders sagged. "Nothing. Neville won't listen to me, anyway. He's gone too far, and he can't come back from this. He's probably hoping I'm dead." A deep frown carved up her forehead. "Do you think he knows Cody and I escaped the lab?"

"Who knows? But what we do know is that he doesn't seem to be trying to save you."

"That's true." She tilted her head side to side, maybe trying to release a knot in her neck. "We'll do this your way. Tell me the plan."

"Good. Once I'm in position, I'll wave to you. Do not move until then, okay?"

She took the binoculars from me and threaded the strap over her neck.

"You're going to sneak into the river upstream a bit, and drift down to the boat." I handed her my knife. "At the jetty, cut the tether, then use the boat to block yourself from their view and drift downstream to me. I'll swim out to you, and we get the hell out of here."

She cocked her head. "You make it sound easy."

"The easiest plans are the best ones."

"I was being sarcastic."

The worry in her eyes demanded that I crush her to my chest and tell her everything would be okay. But this situation wasn't okay, and nothing would be until she was on that rescue chopper and getting the fuck out of here.

I cupped her cheek, and she leaned into my palm.

"You can do this, Layla. And don't worry." I tapped my rifle. "If any of those assholes give you trouble, it will be the last thing they do."

"The goal is to not kill anyone," she said.

"Wrong. The goal is to get that boat so we can catch our ride home." I stood and dragged her up to me.

She wrapped her arms around me. "Thank you."

"Don't thank me until we're out of this mess."

"I'm thanking you for believing in me."

I squeezed her to my body. I would do anything for this woman. I would willingly die for her. Hopefully, it wouldn't come to that, not when I'd started to imagine us having a future together.

We eased apart, and her gaze flitted between my lips and my eyes. Hoping I read her signals right, I kissed her. She melted toward me, opening her mouth, and kissing me in a way that stole every thought from my mind.

Moaning, she pressed her hand on my chest, pushing back. "Let's do that again when we're in that boat together."

I grinned. "Deal." I kissed her forehead. "Stay focused on that boat and let me worry about everything else. This is a good plan, Layla."

"I know. I trust you."

My heart swelled with those words. "Watch for my signal, then head for that boat fast, but in stealth mode."

She saluted me. "Yes, sir."

It took everything I had to leave her. I sprinted through the thick jungle until my lungs burned and sweat poured down my face. All I could think about was Layla—her safety, her smile. Everything about her.

The scars on my back and hip ached with each stride, but I pushed through the pain.

Gasping for breath, I reached the rocky outcrop, and crouching low, I peered through my rifle scope to survey the old church, the jetty, and the bushes where I'd left Layla. Six forty-four-gallon drums were arranged haphazardly beside the church. Flames licking from the tops of them cast an eerie glow across the rough ground nearby. Whoever was cooking something over those barrels had better stay inside or they were toast. The stink of that smoke drifted my way, making my stomach churn with dread. At least I knew the source of the smoke.

I found her amongst the dense bushes, staring right at me.

Now it's up to me to protect her.

I waved a hand over my head. She gave me a quick nod, lowered the binoculars to her chest, and disappeared back into the underbrush.

I spotted her making her way toward the river. She moved like a shadow, silent and determined. My heart swelled with pride and fear in equal measure.

"That's it, Layla, keep going," I whispered, wishing she could hear me.

It killed me that I wasn't with her, protecting her every step of the way. But my role was here, watching over her from afar, and I would kill any fucker that got in her way. My sudden departure from my Navy SEAL career might have left me scarred and broken, but I would use every skill in the book, dirty or not, to keep her safe.

"Come on, Layla." My grip tightened on my rifle. "You've got this."

I steadied my breathing as I peered through the scope on my rifle, watching Layla's movements. She snuck through the bushes toward the river in stealth mode, and my heart thundered in my chest like a fucking jackhammer.

Focus, Hunter. Focus. My rifle seemed heavier than ever, and the air was so damned hot, I could barely breathe.

As Layla moved closer to the riverbank, sunlight glinted off the water, casting a golden glow on her face. Her jaw was clenched with determination, but her eyes darted all over the place. Her fear just about wrenched my heart out.

Jungle sounds amplified around me. The rushing river. A bird that seemed to be screeching right in my fucking ear.

My mind raced with worst-case scenarios. Jaguars. Electric eels. Armed men seeing Layla's dash for the river.

"Keep moving, Layla." My teeth ground together as I gripped the rifle tighter. "You're almost there."

My heart jammed in my throat as Layla slipped past a cluster of bushes so damn thick I couldn't see her. Finally, she reached the river's edge. Squatting down, she looked toward me, and I raised my hand, but without the binoculars, I doubted she saw me.

"Get in the water, Layla."

She looked toward the old church.

Holding my breath, I turned my scope to the

building too, and focused on the abandoned church. At least six armed men were inside, all sporting military-grade rifles. I prayed they stayed where they were.

Layla slipped into the murky water until her head was just above the surface. Swimming with the current, she propelled herself toward the boat tied up to the decrepit jetty much faster than I'd expected.

"Good work." My heart pounded in my chest.

The old church loomed ominously at the river's edge. Its crumbling steeple, that had tilted down the side of the roof, cast a long, dark shadow over foliage nearby. That once-sacred building was now a haven for assholes with weapons capable of killing the only woman who was sacred to me. But one wrong move by them and every one of those bastards were dead.

As she neared the boat, her gaze darted around.

The armed men were still out of sight, yet my finger twitched on the trigger, ready to put a bullet through anyone who ruined our plans.

"Almost there." I sucked in a sharp breath. "Just a little bit more."

Finally, Layla surfaced beside the weathered timber fishing boat. It dipped under her weight as she gripped onto the side and sawed at the rope tethering the vessel to the jetty.

Gnawing fear ratcheted up my spine as I scoped the building. This was our danger zone. Armed men could burst from the church at any moment.

I swept my gaze between Layla hacking at the rope and the open door to the decrepit building. "Come on, Layla."

The boat dipped as the rope released.

"Yes." She did it. "Now get the fuck out of there."

My eyes were glued to the scope as Layla kicked the vessel into the current.

But she was struggling. Her feet were splashing too much.

"Shit, Layla. Come on, get away from there." Forcing my gaze to the building was crushing, but I couldn't get distracted.

Tension radiated through me.

As if taunting me, a gust of wind stirred up the flames within the drums, sending sparks into the air. A shiver ran down my spine as a wave of dread consumed me.

"Nearly there. Don't come out now, you fuckers." My finger hovered over the trigger.

My heart leaped into my throat as a man with a stocky figure, salt and pepper hair, and a warped smile stepped out of the church. He strode to the side with the flaming drums and lit a cigarette. It was Neville, the bastard who had sabotaged Layla's work. The temptation to kill him was huge but I forced myself to hold back. Layla didn't want anyone to die. He was just lucky he faced away from her, or her wishes would be denied.

"We're almost out of this." I breathed, feeling a surge of relief. "Go, Layla."

Every second took a minute. Every breath hurt.

I couldn't see Layla, but her splashes were as if dozens of legs were kicking like crazy.

Every ounce of me wanted to take that man down, but I held back. Patience was our only ally in this deadly game.

Another man stepped through the door.

"Shit," I hissed under my breath, my finger itching to pull the trigger. His tattered military clothing hung off his thin frame. His gaunt face was covered in grime and slick with sweat, and his eyes had a wild glint that made me uneasy.

I resisted the urge to put a bullet in his brain, hoping the man wouldn't notice the drifting boat or Layla kicking like mad behind it.

The wooden boat bobbed in the current, its worn paint and patched-up hull blended into the murky water.

"Stop kicking, Layla." My heart boomed in my ears.

The man glanced around lazily before his gaze settled on the boat. A flicker of confusion crossed his face, followed by suspicion. I could practically see the gears turning in his head.

We'd run out of time and luck.

I clenched my jaw, torn between my instinct to protect her and following her wishes.

I tried to suppress the panic rising within me.

"Walk away, dickhead." My voice cracked with dread. "I don't want to kill you."

If it came down to it, I would sacrifice one life to save another. What did that say about me?

As the man slowly reached for the rifle slung over his shoulder, I knew that our fate was no longer in my hands alone.

"Damn it," I muttered, taking aim through the scope of my rifle.

The man's mouth opened with a shout as he raised his rifle to take a shot at the boat.

I pulled the trigger. The deafening crack of gunfire echoed through the air. The man crumpled to the ground, lifeless. I gritted my teeth.

Men in tattered military clothing poured out of the church with their faces twisted in rage.

"Go, Layla," I shouted. "Get a fucking move on!"

The assholes scrambled across the dirt, yelling and reaching for their weapons.

I pulled the trigger, hitting a man square in his chest, and he flew backward.

I fired again, killing another man.

Several men ran back inside including that fucker, Neville.

The sounds of chaos filled the jungle air—shouts, gunfire, and the sickening thuds of bullets slamming into the boat.

CHAPTER 13

LAYLA

Screaming as bullets splintered the boat all around me, I gripped the side of the old fishing vessel and ducked my head lower. The murky waters splashed everywhere as I kicked harder, desperate to get away from the gunfire.

My muscles burned, but I couldn't stop. Hunter needed me.

"Over there!" a shout echoed across the water.

Were they referring to me? Or Hunter?

I couldn't think. I couldn't breathe. I just ducked lower and kept kicking.

Rapid gunfire was like a swarm of angry hornets buzzing around my ears, relentless and unforgiving. Every kick was a battle between desperation and fear.

Hunter's face appeared in my mind. Would I see him again?

I fought against the current, praying that it didn't drag me toward the men hunting me.

Bullets slammed into the boat and motor; chunks of wood flew everywhere. The sound of gunfire boomed in my ears.

Hunter's army rifle fired in quick succession, adding to the chaos, but unlike the erratic shooting by Neville's men, each shot Hunter made seemed to echo with purpose and precision.

Men screamed in sheer agony, but despite that they were still shooting at me, guilt twisted my insides. These men were dying because of me, because of my research, because of Neville and what he did.

It was wrong. So, so wrong.

More shots rang out, their staccato rhythm punctuating my thundering thoughts.

Kicking furiously, I propelled myself toward where Hunter was waiting. Bullets punched into the boat and the river around me. The churning water seemed cold and unforgiving as if daring me to give up. But I couldn't, not when Hunter risked everything to keep me alive.

A bullet whizzed past my ear, and I ducked lower. My heart pounded like a wild animal trying to escape my chest.

I forced my exhausted body to keep moving. The sounds of gunfire grew more distant, and the screams of the attackers began to fade. With each passing second, hope bloomed within me like a fragile flower, daring me to believe that we might escape this nightmare.

Another cry of agony bounced across the water.

Shit! Was that Hunter?

With my heart in my throat, I peered over the edge of the boat, searching the shoreline ahead. Relief turned my legs to rubber and made my kicks nearly useless. Hunter was on one knee, firing toward the jetty I'd just stolen the boat from.

At the old church, a dark silhouette emerged from the shadows and a sickening wave coursed through me at how calm Neville looked. Like he knew we would be killed. My heart pounded as I tried to make sense of what was happening. The man who had been my boss was working with the men trying to kill us.

Bile rose in my throat. He was not just feeding them alcohol. He had corrupted them with much more than that.

Neville had betrayed me, sabotaged my research, and now he was trying to kill me. All for what? Greed? Power? Sacred berries?

As Neville fired at me and Hunter, a twisted cocktail of emotions washed through me: fear, disgust, anger.

A shot whooshed across the water. Neville flew backward. Blood splattered the wall of the church. Neville crumpled to the ground, lifeless.

"Oh, God. Is he dead?"

Nausea burned my stomach and throat as my anger was replaced with sadness. Not for Neville—he deserved what he got—but for the villagers who had fallen victim to Neville's bullshit.

I need to tell everyone what Neville has done.

Adrenaline pumped through my veins as I kicked harder and tried to wrestle the boat in the right direction.

As I neared Hunter, the gunfire became more frantic and the cold Amazon water seeped into my bones, adding to the terror that gripped my body. I pushed on, powered by thoughts of Hunter fighting to survive.

"Layla! keep going." Hunter's deep voice echoed to me, driving me on.

I peered over the edge of the boat again. Hunter had moved closer to the water's edge.

Shit! What's he doing? He has no cover there!

The relentless gunfire ripped into the wooden hull of the boat and thumped into the old motor.

Oh, God. Could the boat sink?

The wild current suddenly took hold of the vessel. I was no longer in charge; the mighty river was. The water churned around me, taking on a life of its own.

Oh, shit. I'm in trouble.

I peered over the boat. "Hunter! Help."

He flicked his rifle around to his back, and as a

bullet pinged off a rock near his feet, he dove into the river.

My heart threatened to burst.

A bullet slammed into the boat, barely an inch from my fingers. Shrieking, I ducked down, but I had to see where Hunter was. And I had to see who was still shooting at us.

Barely able to breathe, I peered over the edge of the boat.

Hunter's strokes across the murky river were powerful and confident. His legs created a tornado of whitewater behind him.

"Come on, Hunter. Swim."

Tiny eruptions of water exploded near him. Bullets!

I shot my gaze toward the jetty, and my eyes locked onto Neville. My stomach churned. Blood stained the front of his shirt near his left shoulder and his arm hung limp. But he was alive and that meant he was never going to give up. He wanted me dead. He wanted Hunter dead too, and Cody.

The boat was near the middle of the river, and Hunter was still several yards away.

Shit! I can't stop the boat. If he doesn't reach me in time, we'll go right past. He'll never catch me.

I twisted my body the other way and kicked like the devil was on my feet, trying to slow the speed of the boat. "Hunter! Hurry!"

I couldn't see him. I couldn't hear him.

Did I miss him?

Hunter suddenly appeared ahead of the boat. My body melted, and I let the current swing my legs the other way. It took all my effort to just hang on. As Hunter tread water, he raised his arms, ready to catch the boat as we drifted to him. His mouth was open, no doubt catching his breath after that frantic swim.

His eyes met mine. A smile lit up his face, and he shook his head like he couldn't believe what he was seeing.

"Got you!" Hunter's strong arms enveloped me as he clutched the boat over my shoulders. "Well done, Layla. You were amazing."

His words filled me with so much joy, I thought I would pass out.

"Let's get out of here." His voice was tense and focused. "Hang on, I'll climb in first."

As the boat drifted downstream, Hunter showed incredible strength and agility as he pulled himself up and into the boat in one swift move.

"I've got you." He reached under my arms, and the rough wood scraped against my battered legs as he hauled me into the boat.

I flopped on top of him like a dead fish and as we huddled together in the bottom of the boat our short, ragged gasps became one.

"Are you okay?" Concern laced Hunter's words as he brushed my wet hair from my eyes.

"Yes." My voice broke with a sob. "I am now. Thank you."

"What you did was amazing." The warmth of his breath whispered across my ear. "You were so brave."

My heart pounded in my chest. "I was just trying to survive."

"But you never gave up. Even when those bullets were punching into the boat and water around you. God, I thought I was going to lose you again." His voice was gruff with emotion as his strong arms enveloped me in a protective embrace.

The chaos around me faded away. It was just me and Hunter, two wounded souls clinging to each other in the midst of a raging river.

I eased back and our eyes locked. My chin dimpled at the love in his eyes.

He scooped my hair around my ear. "Were you hurt?"

I shook my head. "Were you?"

"No. We got lucky." He cupped my cheek and as I leaned into his warm palm, my heart swelled so much I thought it would burst. I'd crossed a bridge that I hadn't even been looking for. A bridge toward love. Hunter had always fascinated me, but now he'd entered my heart. I wanted him like I'd never wanted anything in my life.

Unable to hold back, I pressed my lips to his. He returned my kiss, and as we sunk deep into each other, he curled his warm hand around my neck, holding me to him. Our tongues glided together, our breaths mingled, and a sigh tumbled from my lips at how perfect he was.

Hunter separated first. "Layla, believe me, I'd love to kiss you all day, but—"

"Oh right, yes." It was like a bubble had burst and our deadly situation crashed onto me again. I slid off him onto the rough floor of the boat. "What do we do?"

He sat up, and peering through the scope on his rifle, he studied the old church in the distance. "Son of a bitch. Neville is still alive."

"I noticed. He's wounded, though."

"Good. I hope the fucker bleeds to death." Hunter shuffled to the back of the boat. "Let's get us across the other side."

"I can't believe Neville would do this. He tried to kill me. Us." My voice choked with emotion, but I fought it. "Are all those other men . . . are they dead?"

Hunter leaned over the motor. "For fuck's sake. The motor is riddled with holes."

He pulled on a handle, and a rope whipped right out of the engine. He stumbled backward and just about fell over the side.

"Fuck!" He pegged the handle into the boat.

My stomach twisted into knots.

When is this nightmare going to end?

CHAPTER 14

LAYLA

OUR BULLET-RIDDLED BOAT wouldn't start and didn't have paddles, and now we were trapped in the wild current, racing along a river that would not release us from its claws.

Frustration darkened Hunter's handsome features as he studied the trees on the opposite side of the river that we cruised past. He pulled a plastic bag from his vest, removed his GPS, and scowling, he jabbed a few buttons.

Clinging onto the boat siding, I scanned the dense jungle that loomed along the edge of the river. In the dark shadows amongst the vegetation, anything could be lurking—especially more men with guns. I pulled my hair back into the band that had nearly escaped in the rushing water and pretending I was some kind of superwoman, I said, "We'll just have to swim to shore."

"Yep. We sure do." He studied the GPS and checked the river ahead. "We're coming up to a bend in the river. That's when we'll jump."

Shielding the sun with my hand, I squinted at the million lights twinkling across the water. The river was moving damn fast. If we didn't swim quickly enough, we could be swept downstream in seconds.

"We can do this, Layla." Confidence emanated from his tone. "You already did the hard part with securing this boat."

The boat wobbled as Hunter shuffled toward me. He squeezed my hand. "We'll do this together, okay?"

I nodded.

He winked. "That's my girl."

He believed in me. Pride swelled in me like I'd never felt before and I squeezed his hand, drawing on his strength and praying that I didn't let him down.

As we huddled together, drifting aimlessly in the relentless current, my nerves zinged like hi-tensile wire and impossible questions thumped into my brain like a jackhammer.

What if I don't swim hard enough?

What if Hunter and I get separated and I never see him again?

What if I get attacked by a croc? Or Hunter does?

"The bend is coming up," he said, snapping me from my rotten thoughts. "Get ready to jump."

He put the GPS away and twisted his rifle around

to his back. "When we hit the water, swim as hard as you can. I'll be with you the whole way."

"I will." Swallowing was like trying to shove dirt down my throat.

"Ready." He put one foot on the side of the boat.

I did the same.

"Set." He pointed to the enormous trunk of a tree along the riverbank. "Swim toward that tree."

Panic surged through me. My heart boomed in my chest.

"Jump." He gripped my waist, launching me into the air. My feet hit the river first, and my chest and face slapped the water. I scrambled for the surface.

Hunter grabbed my arm. "Swim, Layla," he yelled in my ear.

Pushing my body to the limit, I curled my arms and kicked my legs like a black caiman was on my tail.

"That's it. Good girl. Keep going." Hunter's words came in fits and bursts, out of time to my frantic rhythm, but he never left my side.

Finally, we reached the shore, and my boots slipped on the muddy bottom. Hunter clutched my hand, dragged me out of the water, and pulled me into his arms. "You are fucking amazing."

Laughing, he kissed the top of my head and my heart soared like a released balloon.

Between my ragged breaths, I whispered, "So are you."

Hunter helped me to stand and as he pulled out his GPS and checked our position, I studied the surrounding bushes.

"Hunter, look." I pointed at a yellow orchid about twelve feet up a tree. "It's a vanilla orchid."

"That's nice, Layla, but not helpful."

"It is, actually. I know where we are." Squelching in my wet boots, I stepped toward it.

"You do?"

"Yes, I've seen that flower before. Come on." I shoved through a shrub. "If I'm right, the jetty we use for the lab is around the bend."

"Shit, really? You mean we could've stayed on the boat?"

"I think so." I picked up my speed, rushing through the dense bushes along the riverbank.

"Let me go first." Hunter pushed in front of me and barged over and through the plants like a rhino. "I hope you're right."

I spotted another plant I recognized. "There. Look, it's the *Passiflora edulis*."

"Bless you." Hunter grinned.

I laughed. "I've seen this passionflower plant dozens of times. We're nearly at the lab."

Hunter burst through the bushes and onto a path. "Yes."

"See? I told you." I turned toward the river and could just see the jetty through the bushes. I turned the opposite way. "The lab is along here."

Hunter squeezed our palms together. "Let's go."

As we ran along the track, he kept glancing skyward and I imagined he was searching for our rescue helicopter.

I hope we haven't missed it.

Hunter skidded to a stop, and I crashed into his back. He dragged me down to squat next to him and put his finger over his lips.

Ahead of us was the clearing, and beyond that was my research lab where I'd lived and worked for the last eleven months. But the lab was ruined. The screens that had surrounded the front half of the building had been sliced open. The front door had been ripped right off. Inside, tables and chairs were smashed.

A knot swelled in my throat so big I could barely breathe.

Hunter must have decided it was safe to move because he grabbed my hand and strode into the clearing.

He paused at a section of land where the sky was visible and looked upward.

I stepped through the broken doorway to the research facility and crunching over glass, shattered crockery, and scattered cutlery, I entered the hallway. I turned into my test center and my breath choked in my throat as I stared at my ruined lab. The floor was covered in broken equipment. My computer was where I'd last seen it on the floor with all the keys scattered around. Nothing was left in the refrigerated cupboard, and all my samples and scientific equipment were destroyed.

I slumped against the wall, covered my hands over my face, and wept.

"Hey, come here." Hunter held me to his chest and as I cried he didn't say a word.

When I couldn't cry anymore, I eased back, wiping my eyes. "Sorry."

"No need to be."

I wiped the back of my hand under my nose. "God, I must look a mess."

He glided my hair away from my forehead. "You look beautiful."

I chuckled. "Liar."

"You always look beautiful."

"Oh, Hunter." I sucked in a shaky breath. "You're going to make me cry again."

He shrugged a shoulder. "I mean it, Layla. You're the most beautiful woman I've ever met, both inside and out."

I stepped into his embrace and as I listened to his heartbeat through his chest, he ran his hand over my back.

"I've missed you." I sniffed.

He seemed to melt. "I've missed you too."

Easing back, I peered into his amazing blue eyes. "Take me home, Hunter."

His lean, muscular face morphed into the most

glorious smile I'd ever seen. "I thought you'd never ask."

Clutching my hand, he led me from my ruined research lab and out to the clearing.

He'd stacked a pile of timber up and lit a fire. "Hopefully, the smoke will lead the chopper to us before any more of those assholes figure out where we are."

I nodded. "You're so clever."

He threw a couple more planks from the ruined front door onto the fire, then draped his arm over my shoulder. "All we can do now is wait."

I followed the steady stream of smoke up to the sky. "Do you think Cody and your friends are okay?"

"Of course." His confidence was unwavering.

He carried over a log for us to sit on and although I couldn't miss the strength in his arms, I also didn't miss the pain on his face. He lived with pain every single day because of the scars left by his burned skin.

His ongoing agony was the reason I wanted my research to be a success. And for my sister.

He presented the log to me like he was presenting a golden throne. As he snapped a couple more bits of timber off the broken door, I prepared to tell a story that I had never told anyone.

Sitting beside me, he followed a line of smoke up through the gap in the jungle canopy above us. "We can practically send smoke signals to them now."

Grinning, he wriggled his brows, then the smile fell from his face. "What's wrong?"

I settled my hand above his knee. "I owe you a story."

Frowning, he cocked his head.

I cleared my throat. "When I was fifteen, I was a bit of a rebel."

He chuckled. "You? I doubt it."

I huffed. Telling this story made me uncomfortable, and yet at the same time, telling the story to Hunter seemed so perfect.

"I was. I wanted to be like the neighborhood boys. I did skateboarding, rode a BMX, and went fishing. All that stuff. I was bulletproof."

Hunter nodded. "I know that feeling."

"Yes, I'm sure you do." I nudged my shoulder to his. "My sister, Sophia—"

At the mention of her, he squeezed my hand. Maybe he recognized how hard it was for me to reveal the event that changed my sister and me forever.

I released a slow breath. "Sophia and I had a cubbyhouse in a Scarlet Oak tree in our parents' backyard. She was just eleven years old, and I . . . I was acting like a fool. I lit a cigarette. I was showing off, pretending I knew how to smoke, but I dropped the cigarette."

I closed my eyes, picturing what happened like it

was in slow motion, when in reality, it all happened so fast.

"A fire took hold so quickly, trapping us." A tear spilled down my cheek and I flicked it away. "By the time my father dragged us through a hole he chopped in the side of the cubby, Sophia suffered severe burns to the back of her left leg. The agony she was in . . . I can still remember her screams."

He went to put his arm over my shoulder. "Oh, Layla, it wasn't your—"

"No, Hunter. Don't say it wasn't my fault. It was. Sophia suffered horrific burns because of my stupidity, and I didn't even get a scratch. To this day, she has a limp that's a permanent reminder of what I did."

"It was an accident."

"One that should never have happened."

"That's why they are called accidents, Layla. You didn't deliberately light that fire or hurt your sister."

I clenched my fist, digging my nails into my palm. "I deliberately lit that cigarette, knowing it was wrong."

He turned his gaze back to the fire. "Now I understand why you came down here and why you're obsessed with making the burns ointment formula. You have done everything you can to make up for your mistake."

"You're wrong. Nothing makes up for that." I swallowed the lump in my throat.

He threaded his fingers into mine. "Has your sister forgiven you?"

My shoulders slumped. "She says she has but . . ."

He frowned. "But what, Layla?"

"But how can she, really? My stupidity ruined her life."

"Did it? She was only eleven at the time. Her life wasn't mapped out. Things happen that send us in directions we never saw coming. Like us sitting here. I thought I'd lost you forever, but now . . ." He swept his gaze to me. "Now I hope you agree with me that we have something going on. Something special, and real."

"Oh, Hunter. Despite everything that's happened, I feel like I'm the luckiest woman in the world."

"You know, we could have averted all this if you'd just stayed in Yellowstone."

I cocked my head. "Maybe I would have stayed if you'd asked me on a date."

He blinked like he was trying to turn back time. "Are you serious?"

I shrugged. "I don't know, but I kept thinking you were close to asking me out, but each time you pulled back."

He lowered his gaze to his right hand, where a tiny burn scar had stamped its mark below his wrist. "I didn't think you would want to be with a man like me."

186

"What? You mean a brave soldier with a kind soul who makes me laugh and feel like a giddy teenager?"

A tiny smirk curled across his gorgeous lips. "I meant a hideously disfigured and broken man who is no longer a Navy SEAL."

"I don't even see your scars, Hunter. I see you. The real man beneath your skin. And although I love that you dedicated your life to saving people in the navy, if you hadn't left the military the way you did, then we may never have met. So to me, it's a bit of a double-edged sword. Besides, it sounds like you're still saving lives. Case in point." I slapped my chest. "And doing other active missions, and you have your amazing dogs that you train. Maybe I could come and meet some of your dogs when we get back."

His expression twisted like he was trying to hold back a massive grin. "Are you asking me on a date?"

I burst out laughing. "If that's what it takes to get you to realize that I want to be with you, then yes. Mr. Hunter Black, will you go out with me?"

He curled his arm around my neck and planted his lips on my temple. "I thought you'd never ask."

I ran my hand along his thigh. "Is that a yes?"

"Yes. Absolutely yes." He stiffened beside me and whispered, "We have company, to your right."

I snapped my gaze to the edge of the clearing and gasped. "Yamania."

Letting go of Hunter's hand, I stood and took a tentative step toward her.

I wished I could talk to her and tell her how sorry I was.

When she didn't flee, I took another step.

"I'm so sorry," I said even though I knew she didn't understand me. I shook my head, hoping the emotions twisting up my insides conveyed my sincerity.

She gave me a slight nod, then offered a purple orchid flower toward me.

Tears pooled in my eyes as I closed the distance to her. My throat was so swollen with sorrow that I could barely breathe as I accepted the flower from her. "Thank you."

As she nodded, her gaze lowered to my arms.

"I'm sorry for what happened to Na-lynied and your jungle. I'm so, so sorry."

She pointed at one of my many cuts along my forearm.

I brushed my fingers over an inch-long cut that was still bright red. "Yes. I've been through a bit of trouble."

I showed her my right leg which was patterned with cuts and bruises.

Yamania's eyes darkened.

"It's a long story," I said, barely able to comprehend what I'd been through since I last saw her.

Yamania walked away, vanishing within the bushes.

Releasing a sigh, I sniffed the orchid flower she'd

given me, but like many orchids, while this one was beautiful, it didn't have a pleasant scent. I turned toward Hunter and offered a lopsided smile. "She's gone."

"That didn't go so bad though." He opened his hands like he was giving a peace offering.

"At least she didn't try to spear me again."

Hunter nodded over my shoulder, and I turned around. Yamania was back. In her hand was a plant with small, pale green leaves that she'd pulled from the ground, roots and all. She pointed at the grass, and it took me a couple of seconds to understand that she wanted me to sit.

When I sat down, Yamania broke a few leaves off the plant, and as she rubbed them in her palms, she bit off a chunk of the dirt-covered root and chewed it. She spat the chewed-up root into her hands and mixed it with the leaves, then squatting at my side, she used her finger to paint the olive-colored paste over the cuts on my legs.

Tears pooled in my eyes at her tenderness. After everything I'd done to her and her village and her jungle home, this beautiful soul still wanted to help me.

I glanced at Hunter, and he gave me a knowing nod.

Yamania brushed more of her herbal remedy over the cuts on my arms.

I had no idea what the name of the plant was that

she was using on my wounds, and for the first time since I'd arrived in this jungle environment, I didn't want to know. These beautiful people deserved to have their pristine home remain unspoiled and sacred.

Some secrets were better left untouched.

My ointment would help so many people, but at what cost?

The people in the Manouthiciara tribe did not need nor want my ointment, or any Western products, ruining their lives. I'd achieved what I'd come here to do: make an ointment that would heal burned skin. But the formula for that ointment was a secret I would never reveal.

A thumping beat shattered our reverie. I glanced at the sky.

Jumping back, Yamania gasped.

"It's okay," I said, pushing up from the ground.

Covering her ears, Yamania sprinted into the bushes and disappeared.

That would be the last time I ever saw her or any of her family.

I strode to Hunter and threaded my arm around his waist.

His face lit up with a beautiful grin. "Here come the boys."

As he hugged me to his side and beamed his massive smile up at the open sky, a sense of calm washed over me.

At the same time, I wanted the world to know what Neville had done. I vowed that nobody would repeat the atrocities he had leveled on this native environment.

Did he survive that bullet wound?

I needed to find out, because if he did, we had to remove him from this place and make him pay for endangering lives.

CHAPTER 15

HUNTER

THE BRUTAL DOWNDRAFT from the chopper blade whipped a tornado through the dense jungle around us and swirled the smoke into a frenzy.

My buddy, Gunn, leaned out the side of the chopper, and I waved. He too was an ex-Navy SEAL and just like me, Gunn bore burn scars from that aircraft carrier accident. But the poor bastard had a nasty scar on his face. At least I didn't have that.

"Here we go, Layla. Stand back," I yelled over the thudding chopper blades, pulling her to the edge of the clearing.

Gunn whipped down the winch line like a pro, touching down a few yards from the fire.

I strode to him. "Boy, am I glad to see you."

"Likewise."

We clapped each other's backs.

"Where are Booker and Wyatt?" His scowl flicked between Layla and me.

"They're in the first chopper. We crashed into a tree, and the chopper got trapped sixty feet in the air."

"Son of a bitch." His eyes filled with dread as if he expected the worst. "What's their status?"

"They survived the crash, but Booker's legs were pinned in the wreckage. We need to cut him free."

"Let's get moving then." Gunn unhooked a harness from his hip and turned to Layla. "Layla, I assume?"

She nodded with a small smile. "Yes. I'm sorry about all this trouble."

"Trouble?" He cocked his head at me. "This is nothing, right, Hunter?"

Chuckling, I helped Layla into the harness. "Who's our pilot?"

"Xavier." Gunn tightened the harness around Layla's waist.

"Good. We're going to need his expertise."

Xavier was practically born in a pilot seat.

"See you in a sec, buddy." He nodded at me.

I rested my hand on Layla's shoulder. "Don't fall out of the chopper this time."

She tilted her head at me. "No way."

"Okay, Layla, hang onto here." Gunn indicated to a shoulder strap on his harness.

She did as he asked, and he waved at the chopper.

Layla's eyes met mine before she was winched from the Amazon jungle for a second time. As the blades whirred overhead, casting a menacing shadow on the jungle floor, I stepped back to watch her ascent. My heart clenched over what she'd been through. None of this was her fault. All her hard work, and she had nothing to show for it.

Her computer!

As Gunn manipulated her into the chopper, I sprinted back into the ruined lab and snatched the laptop from the floor. I tried to snap it shut but the frame was buckled, and the keys were gone. But with a bit of luck, the hard drive wouldn't be ruined, and Wyatt could work his magic on it and salvage something for Layla after all.

The winch returned to the ground for me. I hooked it to my vest, and gripping the laptop under my arm, I gave Gunn, who was leaning out the chopper, the *all-clear* signal.

The helicopter blades roared above me, drowning out the relentless jungle sounds and my burn scars stung like a bitch as I was hauled into the bird. Layla's scars were mental ones, and she'd fought hard to eradicate them by providing a solution to her sister's burn wounds. But her sister's burn scars would be there to stay, just like mine. Layla knew that, yet she had persisted anyway.

I fought my agony by scanning the jungle below

searching for tangos and wondering why Neville had sabotaged her work.

Gunn pulled me into the chopper and grabbing onto a handle, I shuffled inside, then leaned toward the cockpit. "Hey, Xavier, thanks for saving our asses."

"The pleasure is all mine." Xavier saluted me from the pilot seat.

As Gunn secured the winch, I showed Layla her laptop. "Thought you might need this."

Her expression twisted into a baffling mix of confusion and delight.

I shoved the computer into a duffle bag secured on the opposite seat to Layla and pulled on a headset. "Let's go get the rest of our team."

"Roger that," Xavier said. "You got some directions for me?"

He raised the chopper away from the tree canopy.

I pulled the GPS from my vest, gave him the coordinates and as the helicopter banked sharply, I rested my hand on Layla's thigh. "You okay?" I yelled over the thumping beat of the rotors.

She nodded, but a sadness washed over her that was like a punch to my gut. She'd been through so much.

Dragging my eyes from her, I explained to Gunn and Xavier how our chopper went down, the angle of the wreck, and how Booker's legs were pinned.

"You two better figure out how to get him out of

there ASAP," Xavier said. "We don't have enough juice to mess around."

"Roger that." I nodded at Gunn. "I don't suppose you brought a hydraulic spreader with you?" I joked. It would be handy to have the 'jaws of life' with us.

Gunn shuffled to the equipment box at the back and pulled out a crowbar. "That's a start."

I took the crowbar from him. "What do we have to cut metal?"

He pulled out plyers, a hammer, and a screw-driver. "We're gonna need a bigger knife than this though."

I took the utility knife. "We could use the winch to pry the metal apart?"

Gunn clicked his fingers and pointed at me. "Good plan."

"Almost there," Xavier called from the cockpit.

Layla touched a blue, swollen lump on her thigh. Her legs were covered in cuts and bruises, as were her arms. But she got damn lucky they were her only injuries.

"I see them," Xavier hollered from the cockpit and pointed forward.

Leaning out the side of the chopper, I peered across the sea of green to a stream of red smoke drifting from the dense trees ahead.

"That'll be Wyatt," I said. "He must've heard us coming."

"I'll circle around the crash site," Xavier said.

Layla gripped her seat until her knuckles turned white. Being in a chopper with open doors was not for everyone.

Her gaze met mine, and I mouthed, *Are you okay?*

She nodded, but the fear in her eyes said otherwise.

As Xavier circled our helicopter around the crash site, Wyatt leaned out the wreck and gave us a wave.

"That's a good sign," Gunn said.

"Sure is. Let's get them the hell out of here. You grab the gear." I nodded at Gunn. "I'm lowering down first, and I'll relay a plan."

"Copy that." He handed me a comms device.

As Xavier maneuvered the bird over the top of the wreck, I guided the comms around my neck, turned it on, and attached the winch to my vest. "You hear me?"

"Loud and clear," Xavier called. "You ready?"

"Roger that." I gripped onto the hook and the winch lowered me onto the wreck.

The path the chopper had taken was easy to see as it left an erratic line of broken tree branches in its wake.

"You made it," Wyatt called as he hauled me into the wreck.

"It wasn't easy, I'll tell ya." The chopper creaked beneath my weight as we shook hands.

"How you doing, Cody?" Bracing to counterbalance the steep angle of the floor, I squatted at Cody's side.

"I'm good now that you're here." The bruising on his face looked like he'd lost a boxing match. His left eye was swollen shut and the strip of fabric that had been tied around his forehead was stained with blood.

"Let's get you out of here first." I tapped his leg. "We need to get you into this harness. Can you stand?"

As Wyatt and I helped Cody upright, I relayed through my comms to Gunn that Cody was coming up first.

Cody wobbled on unsteady legs as we hooked him into the harness.

"Okay, Gunn, bring him up."

I held onto Cody until the tension on the winch was ready, then eased him out of the wreck. With Cody under control, I turned my attention to Booker. "Hey, captain, how you doing?"

"I could use a beer, that's for sure." Booker had brutal bruising and cuts on the left side of his face, but other than his pinned legs, he seemed fine.

"I reckon we could arrange that." I scanned the maze of twisted metal and shattered glass around him. We got damn lucky to survive this crash. Leaning against the wall to get my balance, I studied the section of the wreck trapping Booker's legs. "Can you feel your feet?"

"Yep. And I can wriggle my toes." His face was pale and drawn, and despite his words, his tone suggested that he was in some serious pain.

"Good. We'll get you out of here in no time."

"Hunter, Cody is secure." Gunn's voice boomed in my comms. "What do you need?"

"Bring down those tools, the harness, and attach it to a rope for Booker. I think we'll have to go with the plan of using the winch."

"Roger that. I'm on my way."

I tapped Booker's arm. "Gunn's on his way down. Sit tight."

"Okay, I'll just wait here then." Booker cracked a crooked smile.

I shuffled into the back.

"You guys had any trouble?" I asked Wyatt.

"Just a few monkeys checking us out. What about you?"

I shook my head. "We've been through hell. Wasn't sure we'd make it in time."

"I knew you would. You've never let us down before."

Frowning, I nodded at him. "Thanks. I've got one hell of a story to tell you guys, though."

Gunn lowered down on the winch, and we pulled him into the wrecked chopper. As he unhooked the winch, he whistled. "Holy hell, you guys sure know how to make a mess of things."

He shook Wyatt's hand and shuffled toward Booker.

I explained to Wyatt my plan to use the winch to pry away the metal pinning Booker's legs in the cockpit.

He nodded. "Sounds good. I've been trying to shift that metal since you left, and the only way it will budge is if you lift it from the outside."

"Then that's what we'll do." I grabbed the winch. "I'll crawl over the outside. You guys work inside and hook this on when I pass it through to you."

Wyatt nodded. "Roger that. Don't fall off. I hear it's a long way to the bottom."

I chuckled. It was still hard to believe Layla survived the fall.

As I climbed out the chopper, the giant trees surrounding the wreck shuddered with the down-draft from the chopper hovering overhead.

The angle of the wreck meant every movement I made over the outside was a battle against gravity. Thankfully, none of the chopper blades had remained intact during the crash, so I was able to crawl across the roof to the cockpit.

Gripping onto the edge of the shattered wind-shield, I leaned inside. "Find a section of metal to hook this on."

I fed the winch hook through to Wyatt.

As Wyatt secured the hook to the metal pinning Booker's legs, I studied his position. He was still strapped into the pilot seat. He'd spent the last twenty hours in that position, facing toward the jungle floor below. When we unpinned his legs from the wreck, there was a good chance he would be too stiff to move.

Gunn nodded at me. "Hook is ready."

Fearing the winch would come free and rip my bloody head off, I eased back and braced myself against the giant tree that had halted the chopper's plummet to the ground.

I glanced up at Xavier through the glass in the cockpit floor of the chopper above us. "Okay, Xavier, pull the winch up, slow and steady."

"Roger that."

The downdraft hit us like we were inside a tornado.

And the roaring engine above us obliterated all sound. Yet as the winch started to pull, metal screeched loud enough to hear over the noise.

Come on. Come on.

The metal slowly gave way, buckling and crumbling as the hook peeled a slab off Booker.

A loud metallic twang echoed about the bushes and the entire wreck jolted downward.

"Fuck!" I gripped a branch as thick as my thigh.

The wreck jolted again.

"Shit! It's gonna go!" Gunn yelled through our comms.

I looked up to the bird. "Xavier, stop. Stop!"

The winch halted.

Gunn looked at me from behind the pilot's seat.

I huffed a massive breath. "Can you release your legs, Booker?"

His face contorted with agony as he pushed on the twisted metal over his thighs, trying to wriggle free.

Finally, he met my gaze and shook his head.

"Xavier, send down the second winch," I said.

"Roger that." As a second winch and hook lowered toward us, Layla leaned out the open door of the chopper. Her hair whipped around her face. Her mouth was open, but I couldn't hear a single word.

"Gunn, grab that winch and hook yourselves on. If this wreck goes you're gonna need it."

"But what about Booker?" he said.

I met Booker's gaze. He shook his head and mouthed, *leave me.*

"No fucking way!" I yelled. "If this thing goes, I'll take Booker. Wyatt and Gunn, you two hang onto that other winch and dive out that side, and don't get tangled in this wreck. Understood?"

"Roger that," Gunn said. Then he yelled the instruction again, obviously for Wyatt's benefit.

I stepped into the harness and attached the rope connecting to the chopper above. Pushing off the tree, I gripped onto the side of the shattered windshield, reached into the cockpit, and threaded the rope connected to my harness around Booker's body, under his arms.

"What are you doing, Hunter?" Booker yelled.

"Saving your ass. Undo your seatbelt and grab my vest."

Booker either didn't have the energy to argue or knew there was no point because there was no way I would give up.

Once his seatbelt was released, his body slumped forward. He was too weak to fight gravity.

"What are you doing, Hunter?" Gunn glared at me.

He knew exactly what I was doing. It was fucking dangerous. If Xavier had to do a sudden evasive maneuver, I was duckshit.

"Move your asses, guys. We don't have much time," Xavier said, urgency clear in his voice.

"Copy that." I focused on the wreckage pinning Booker down.

"This is a bad idea, Hunter," Booker yelled in my ear.

"Stop your whining and get ready." I tied the rope off at the front of his chest. "Just make sure your head doesn't get near this rope. Understood?"

"Copy that." Booker clamped his jaw.

"Let's try this again." My heart hammered in my chest. I nodded at Wyatt and Gunn. "You two get ready to move. Xavier, try the first winch again, slow and steady."

"Roger that."

The cable attached to the hook around the twisted metal pulled again. Peeling off like the lid on a sardine can, the metal screeched.

A loud crack boomed. Booker's bloodshot eyes glared at me.

The wreck jolted downward six inches. Booker cried out and flopped forward.

"He's free!" I yelled. "Get out. Get out."

The wreck jerked down again. The rush of blood to Booker's body rendered him unconscious. I hooked my hands under his armpits.

The metal screeched.

The wind howled around us.

The fucking wreck dropped another four inches.

"Fucking wait, you bitch," I screamed.

I wrestled Booker's body out of the pilot seat.

"Booker. Booker," I screamed, but he was out cold.

The wreck dropped again. I pulled Booker's dead weight toward me. Every twist of my torso drove spears of pain through my scars. I gritted my teeth, forcing my body through the pain.

The wreck released an almighty groan. Shrieking my fury, I hauled Booker out the shattered cockpit window. The wreck plunged from the trees, and Booker and I dangled from the rope like a pair of dead fish.

"Holy fuck, Hunter. You've got nine lives, man," Gunn said in my ear.

I looked up. Gunn and Wyatt cheered as they dangled on the second winch.

Despite my agony, I grinned at them like I'd won the fucking lottery.

Gunn and Wyatt were lifted into the chopper first, and as I waited my turn, I said to Booker, "You're gonna be okay, Booker. You'll be okay."

His silent reply carved a hole in my heart.

It's just a blood rush. That's all it is.

We were hauled up to the chopper, and Booker was pulled in first. As he flopped onto the floor of the chopper, I unhooked from the harness and kneeled at his side.

"Booker," I shook his shoulders.

He rolled his head toward me. "Stop yelling at me."

His eyes flickered open.

We burst out laughing. Hot damn, it felt good.

"Take us home, Xavier," I yelled in my comms.

He responded by tilting the chopper like it had been released from a slingshot.

I glanced at Layla, expecting to see relief and her glorious smile. But I didn't see either. The last few days of hell were painted over her body, but the depth of sadness in her eyes showed how broken she was.

Layla was a good woman, trying to do good things. Instead, she was left with a failed project and a long list of unanswered questions.

I leaned into her ear. "You okay?"

She nodded, but her sadness betrayed her.

"What's wrong? Is it Neville?"

The depth of her sorrow grew deeper as she nodded. "I hate that he's staying here. And he should pay for endangering lives."

"You're assuming he survived that bullet wound."

She nodded. "That's true."

As I looked into Layla's troubled eyes, something shifted inside me. I would do anything to take away her sorrow. And in that instant, I knew I was more than just attracted to Layla. I was in love. And I would do anything to prove my love to her.

"Xavier," I hollered into my mic. "We have another person to pick up."

"We do?" both Xavier and Gunn said.

"Yeah. If he's still alive, that is."

As I told them about Neville and directed them to where I thought the abandoned church would be, Layla smiled at me through teary eyes.

I just hoped that fucker wasn't dead or Layla may never get her answers.

CHAPTER 16

LAYLA

THE HELICOPTER BANKED SHARPLY to the left, nudging me closer to Hunter.

"Thank you," I whispered to him.

He gripped his large hand around mine.

As the helicopter cut through the air, Hunter spoke in his microphone to his team. I couldn't hear what he was saying, but the way Gunn nodded, frowned, and looked at me, I had a feeling Hunter was telling them about Neville shooting at us.

The thud of the helicopter's blades drowned out my thoughts, which was good because I had so much crashing through my brain, I could barely think anyway.

Hunter leaned in closer to me and his hot breath brushed my ear. "Can you believe we walked all that way?"

I shook my head. We didn't just walk; we survived.

Hunter and Gunn shifted to peer out the open doorway, and I leaned forward to look out too. We were following above the muddy brown river that we'd drifted along in the bullet-riddled boat.

The abandoned church came into view, and I gasped at the five lifeless bodies that lay scattered around the church and derelict jetty. Their tattered clothing and dirty militia uniforms were a haunting reminder of their violent attack. A wave of nausea rolled through me. I'd seen some of these men get shot, but seeing them from this view, sprawled out and still, made the reality so much worse.

These deaths were on Neville's head too.

I searched for Neville's body as the pilot circled the building twice, but I couldn't see him. I also couldn't shake the dreadful feeling that more horror was heading our way.

Hunter squeezed my hand and leaned toward me. "We're putting the bird down to see if we can find him. You can stay in here if you want."

I shook my head. "I'm coming with you."

"I figured you'd say that."

The pilot lowered the helicopter onto the small field of rocks next to the river, creating ripples across the water. A short distance away was the jetty I'd stolen the boat from. I'd been so terrified when I'd swum out to that boat, that I could hardly remember doing it.

As the helicopter rotors slowed, Hunter grabbed my hand.

"Keep your head down," he said as he pulled me out and onto the ground.

Crouching over, we raced across the loose rocks, heading toward the old church that was choked by creeper vines.

I froze. Na-lynied, the tribal elder's son whose manly shouts had once echoed through the jungle, lay lifeless among the dead.

My heart ached with sorrow and fury. His death was Neville's fault.

"Oh my god. That's Na-lynied," Cody said. His enormous eyes blazed with distress.

Hunter's team checked the men sprawled on the ground to see if they were alive. None were. They gathered all the weapons and stacked them in a pile. I didn't care what they did with those guns as long as they didn't leave them here. The natives had been successfully living here with primitive weapons since the dawn of time. They didn't need guns like these.

At the front door, Hunter pointed to a trail of blood across the three weathered wooden stairs that led up to a small entrance with several missing planks.

"Come on." Hunter placed his hand on my shoulder. "We need to keep moving."

Blinking away tears, I followed him through the church's open doorway, and it took a couple of beats for my eyes to adjust to the dim light.

The church had been stripped of chairs, and the scent of decay and dampness filled the air.

"Stay sharp," Hunter whispered and gripped his weapon tighter.

Maybe he felt the same dread I did.

Moss covered nearly every surface and a date palm had somehow grown up through the floorboards and angled its trunk out the window to keep thriving. Sunlight speared through a crack in the roof and beamed onto the toppled altar.

Neville was slumped on the floor against it. Blood seeped from a bullet wound in his chest. His breaths were shallow, each one a painful struggle.

But it wasn't his near-death state that shocked me; it was the makeshift laboratory surrounding him.

"Wh-what the hell?" Cody stammered as he walked toward the tables.

Steering away from Neville, I strode to a row of test tubes and lab equipment. Bunches of my precious berries were scattered across the table, and their shriveled flesh confirmed they weren't fresh. But it was the large glass tank that housed dozens of giant green frogs that had me gasping. *Was he using the frogs to test his burns ointment? Was that what the fires in the drums were for?* Oh god, nausea wobbled in my stomach.

Marching back to Neville, I stared into his blood-shot eyes. "What the hell are you up to?"

Neville breathed in a raspy breath and his eyes darted to Hunter's rifle.

"Answer me!" My voice quivered with fury. "What are you doing with my berries and those frogs?"

His breath wheezed and his eyes rolled.

"Neville," I spat his name. "Are you testing your burns ointment on frogs? Is that it?"

Neville released a wet breath. "I don't care about some fucking burns ointment."

I jerked back snapping my gaze to the berries and frogs. "What? You told me that's why you're here. . . in the Amazon. What are you doing then?"

I kicked his foot, and he gasped like I'd kneed him in the head. "People died because of you, natives, our friends."

He shifted his gaze from me to Hunter and his lips twisted into a bitter snarl. "Do you have any idea what the toxins from those frogs can do?"

Dread crashed through me like a tidal wave. "Oh, my fucking god. You're making hallucinogenic drugs? Is that it?"

"I'm making a lot of people rich, Layla. And happy." Red bubbles spilled over his lip.

"What the fuck, Neville?" It took all my strength to resist punching him in the throat. "Why did you try to kill us?"

A bloody dribble spilled down his chin. "I need those berries?"

I shot a glance at Cody then peering back at Neville, I frowned. "What for?"

He shrugged, then gasped in agony and pressed a hand over his bloody bullet wound.

He's in pain. Good.

"What do you need the berries for!" I yelled in his face.

"The frogs. . . it's their favorite."

"You pathetic bastard. You wanted us dead so we couldn't share our Inocea Berry Ointment. Is. . . is that it?" I struggled to comprehend this was happening.

His bloodshot eyes seemed to look through me. "I'm a better scientist than you'll ever be."

I shuddered my fury.

"Let's go." Hunter wrapped his hand around my arm, pulling me away.

I yanked my arm free. "You're not a scientist. You're a murderer. Innocent people like Na-lynied died because of you. And you tried to kill me, Neville."

A bloody globule slipped down his chin.

"Who else is involved? You didn't do this alone. You're not smart enough." Out the corner of my eye, Wyatt and Gunn sifted through the lab equipment.

"Fuck you. This frog drug is my creation. All

mine." A weird smile crossed his lips, and he coughed a bloody breath.

"Bullshit. If you don't tell me who helped you, I'll let you die right here." I clenched my fists and jaw, hoping he fell for my bluff. As much as I hated him, I didn't want his death on my conscience.

"Neville." I squatted at his side. "Don't let them get away with this. Tell me who helped you."

"Layla, we have to go." Hunter squeezed my wrist.

"Wait," I snapped. "He's working with someone. I need to find out who."

"Let's roll." Wyatt's voice bounced off the moss-covered walls.

I tried not to cringe as I placed my hand on Neville's chest. "Hey, come on, don't you want to do the right thing?"

My heart boomed in my chest as his eyes fixed on me, but as the light faded from his irises, my miniscule opportunity to obtain answers slipped away.

My world melted around me.

Hunter lifted me to my feet.

"That bastard was working with someone," I yelled.

Hunter wrapped me in a bear hug. "We'll find out who."

"You're damn right we will." I pulled out of his grip and raced to the tables and equipment. "There must be clues here. Quick, Cody, search his stuff."

"Anyone have a camera?" Hunter called out.

"I do." Gunn held up his cell phone.

"Good. Take photos of everything—Neville's body, the lab, frogs, berries, those soldiers outside. We need all the evidence we can get."

As everyone spread out, I rummaged through papers and notepads scattered across the table, but I couldn't stop looking at all those poor frogs.

"Cody, we have to release these frogs, help me." I raced around the other side of the table and reached into the tank.

"Layla, stop!" Cody yelled. "They're poisonous."

I yanked my hand out. "Shit. Help me carry the tank outside."

Hunter groaned like he'd swallowed a coconut whole. "Move aside." He shoved me backwards. "Wyatt, help out here."

As Hunter and Wyatt carried the tank outside, my hands shook with anger and fear. Did Neville really do this on his own?

Determined to find out, I shuffled through his paperwork, trying to make sense of Neville's messy handwriting. There had to be something here that would lead me to whoever he was working with.

"Hey, look what I found." Cody pulled a clunky laptop from beneath a stack of papers.

I'd never seen it before, but my heart raced. *Does that have the answers I want?*

"That'll do." Hunter appeared at my side. "Frogs are free, and we have to go. Now."

I took one more glance around the messy lab, but as Hunter tried to drag me away, my gaze fell on Neville's lifeless body.

"Hunter, wait."

His troubled gaze pierced me.

"Can we . . .? Would it be possible to take Neville's body with us?"

"Layla! What the fuck?"

"I'm sure his parents would like to bury him properly. It's the right thing to do."

Hunter groaned, then waved over Gunn. "Give me a hand."

Gunn scowled but without argument, he joined Hunter in carrying Neville's body out of the church.

Cody joined my side, and we followed behind. "I can't believe Neville did this. He tried to kill us."

I wrapped my hand over his arm. "I know. I can't believe it either. But I'm going to make it my mission to find out if he was working with someone." I met Cody's gaze. "They can't get away with this."

Cody nodded. "Good. I'll back you up with anything you need."

As we returned to the helicopter where Booker was fast asleep, Hunter and Wyatt loaded Neville's body onto the floor of the chopper and covered his face with a cloth that somehow made him look even worse.

Hunter helped Gunn stack the weapons they'd

taken from the dead men in the helicopter and we had barely strapped in before Xavier lifted off.

I took one last look at the crumbling church and the bodies around it and wondered if that was the end to the unnecessary deaths.

As miles and miles of vegetation crossed beneath us, taking me from my little section of the jungle that I would never see again, more questions flooded my mind than answers.

Was everything I knew about Neville a lie?

Would Yamania and the Manouthiciara tribe recover from what we did?

And what was I going to do with my life now?

CHAPTER 17

HUNTER

WE MADE a short stop at Aeroporto Internacional de Tabatinga, the remote Brazilian airfield near the Colombian border. Although Charlie was happy to see us, and even happier to see Layla and Cody and all the weapons we'd removed from the corrupted natives, he made it well known that he was pissed about us crashing his bird.

But knowing Hank, he would make sure Charlie was well compensated for the inconvenience.

From that airstrip, we bounced through Bogota, Columbia and then toward home. Layla and I dozed on and off during the journey, but the moment our boots touched down in Yellowstone, the weight of the last few days came down on me like an army tank, and I had no idea how Layla was still stringing sentences together.

"Welcome home," I said to Layla.

She barely managed to smile. "Thanks."

I understood her turmoil. On one hand, she was lucky to make it out alive; on the other, everything she'd worked for was ruined.

Two ambulances and police officers met us at the airfield. As Booker and Cody were taken care of by paramedics, we made promises to see them soon.

Neville's body was loaded into the second ambulance and after Layla refused to go to the hospital, the police took Layla and me to the police station where we fielded questions about Neville's death. Layla told them everything Neville had done, and how I'd shot Neville and the other armed men in self-defense when they'd tried to kill us.

It seemed like forever before we were able to leave, and we took a taxi back to Team Eagle headquarters. As I steered Layla inside the vast garage-like space, the familiar smell of oil and metal greeted us as we entered. The interior was lined with high-tech equipment, specialized vehicles, and walls adorned with maps and mission briefings.

It felt like home.

"Hey, Hunter," Xavier called out from across the room, his voice sounding more tired than usual. He leaned against a workbench with his arms crossed over his broad chest.

"They let you out, Hunter?" Wyatt joked as he limped toward me with his hand out. "Thought they would've locked you up and thrown away the key."

Gunn stood beside Wyatt, looking equally weary. "You're one lucky son of a bitch, Hunter."

"Yeah, I know."

"Want a beer?" Wyatt asked. "We're heading over to the pub for a few. I think Colton and Walker will join us."

As much as I would have loved a beer with them and more guys from Team Eagle, I wanted time with Layla more.

"Listen, guys." I stepped closer to them. "Layla and I need some time to . . . process . . .."

"Ahh, *process*. Is that what they call it these days?" Wyatt grinned like a buffoon.

"Funny." I rolled my eyes at him. "But I promise we'll catch up soon, all right?"

"Of course." Xavier slapped my shoulder. "We're just glad it wasn't either of you two that was taken away in that body bag."

Layla eased in beside me. "I can't thank you men enough for saving me and Cody. Without you—"

"Ah, it was nothing," Wyatt said.

"It was more than nothing," she said. "It was everything. You risked your lives to save me, and saying thank you hardly seems enough."

"It's all good." I pulled her to my side. "This is what we do, right, guys?"

As they nodded, Layla leaned into me like she had the weight of the world on her shoulders. That was when I remembered her computer.

"Hey, Wyatt." I plucked Layla's damaged laptop from my bag. "Any chance you could get info off this computer?"

Wyatt whistled. "Holy hell, did this thing have a fight with a buffalo?"

"Just an angry native." Layla shrugged.

"Well, as long as the hard drive isn't damaged, all the data should be there."

Layla's shoulders softened. "That would be amazing."

"And we have this one too." I handed Wyatt the computer we'd found in Neville's dodgy lab in the old church. "See if you can find out who Neville, Layla's boss in the jungle, was sharing intel with."

"Can you also find out if Monarch Medicines who Neville said had funded his research in the Amazon actually exists," Layla said. "I have a feeling that everything he told me was a lie."

Wyatt flipped open the laptop. "Jesus, this thing is a dinosaur."

Layla scooped her hair around her ear. "Any information you can find would be helpful."

"I'll let you know how I go." Wyatt jabbed the start button on Neville's computer.

"Catch you guys later." I turned Layla toward the door.

"Don't do anything I wouldn't do," Wyatt called.

"That doesn't leave a lot." I waved at him over my shoulder.

As I guided Layla toward my truck, although the urge to ask her to come back to my place was huge, I wanted to offer her an easy out, so I asked, "Did you want me to take you home?"

She cleared her throat and scrunched her nose in the cutest of ways. "I never told my parents exactly where my research was because they would never have approved, and I certainly don't want to greet them after eleven months away looking like this." She raised her arms, showing all the cuts and bruises. "I wasn't supposed to be back here for another seven months."

"In that case, you're coming to my place." I opened the truck door and helped her in.

My heart pounded to an excited beat as I raced around to the driver's side.

Grinning at me, she said, "So, is this our first official date?"

I keyed the engine. "I guess it is."

She giggled and as I laughed with her, I drove onto the winding road that passed dense forests and open meadows.

Our conversation was about anything but the Amazon jungle and what had happened there. I told her about Luna, my one-eyed rescue dog.

"Oh, I can't wait to meet her."

"She's going to lick you to death, so be prepared."

"After what we've been through, I think I'm prepared for anything."

As I cruised up my driveway, the view beyond my home was snowy peaks that pierced the sky and yellow pastures that filled the land in between.

My heart swelled with pride as I helped Layla from the truck and led her toward the large fenced-in area filled with obstacle courses and drill equipment.

"Here's where I train the dogs." I pointed at the small arena.

I led her toward the holding pens where a few dogs wagged their tails and jumped against the fence.

"I work with multiple breeds, some specially bred, others rescued from bad situations. This is Neptune." We paused at the German Shepherd's cage. "He's as hyperactive as a Jack Russell, but we're working on that."

"He's beautiful." Layla's eyes sparkled as she scratched his head through the fence.

I soaked in Layla's beauty. Despite everything she'd been through, she was still stunning. When she licked her lips, my damn cock throbbed to attention.

"Right." I turned away from her before the bulge in my jeans couldn't be ignored. "Let me show you around inside."

As I marched away, Layla raced to my side and slipped her hand into mine. Her grip was so natural, like we'd been holding hands for years, and the throbbing in my groin let me know that it felt so damn good.

I pushed open the door, and Luna came bounding toward us. I scooped up the shagpile and ruffled the hair between her floppy ears. "This is Luna."

Luna squirmed in my arms, trying to lick Layla.

"Hello, Luna." Layla giggled as she ran her hand over Luna's back. "What breed is she?"

"She's a bitsa," I said, kissing the top of Luna's head. "Bitsa this and bitsa that. I think she has about six different breeds in her. That's why the poor thing is so confused."

"She doesn't look confused to me. Just happy."

"She is now. She was far from it when I rescued her."

Layla scratched behind Luna's ear, and Luna wagged her tail. "Some people can be so cruel."

"Yeah, gutless bastards." I put her down and Luna jumped up on Layla's leg.

"Not yet, girl. You'll get time with Layla in a minute." I flicked my hand, and Luna came to my side.

I showed Layla around my home and in the bathroom, I plucked a fresh towel from the cupboard. "Here, take all the time you want. I'll rustle us up some food."

Gripping the towel to her chest, she parted her lips like she wanted to say something that was so profound the words couldn't release. Finally, she reached up on her toes and kissed me.

"Thanks, Hunter. Thanks for everything." She gave me a small smile before she stepped back.

"Sing out if you need anything."

As the shower ran, I plucked steaks and veggies from the fridge, and took them out to my barbeque. I heated the grill and as images of Layla's wet, naked body flashed through my mind, my cock grew so hard it was going to punch through my jeans.

Layla made me feel alive, and my nerves zapped all over the place. Yet my emotions were like a yo-yo bouncing between being as horny as a fucking teenager, to the reality check that I was not the man I used to be.

Before my body was turned into a hideous scarred mess, I could walk up to any woman and ask her out.

Now, though, I didn't want anyone to see my ugly wounds.

"Hey."

I spun to Layla's voice. She stood in the doorway wearing nothing but a towel.

"Did you need something?" I swallowed hard, and my cock bounced to life.

Her eyes sparkled and her skin had a red flush from the hot water. Her wet hair spilled over her shoulders, and she looked both refreshed and fucking sexy.

"Yes." Her voice was barely a whisper. "I need you."

My jaw dropped.

"Can you wash my back, please?" She turned and lowered the towel to reveal the line of her back right down to the swell of her glorious ass.

I tried to shift the painful bulge in my pants while she wasn't looking, but it grew bigger.

As she peered at me over her shoulder, her eyes glowed with pure lust as the towel lowered an inch more, revealing the valley between her butt cheeks.

I tossed aside the tongs, turned off the barbeque, and marched to her. "That's a hell yes from me."

Giggling, she gripped my hand and led me to the bathroom.

She stepped into the tumbling water, and as she turned around to give me a mighty fine view of her glorious ass, my cock pounded like a jackhammer.

Calm down, big fella. She just wants her back washed.

I wanted her so bad, I could burst. I wanted to lick the water off her shoulder. I wanted to cup her perky breasts with my hands. I wanted to bury my throbbing cock deep inside her.

But I didn't want her to see me naked.

She glanced at me over her shoulder. "Come on, get your gear off."

I stood at the door like a fucking dumb ass. I couldn't make my feet move.

"Hunter, you can't wash me from there." A stunning smile danced across her lips. "Get in here with me. That's an order."

Barely able to breathe, I stripped off my socks and boots, undid the buckle on my belt, undid my zipper, and yanked down my jeans and undies. My cock bounced toward her like it was a steel rod and she was a giant magnet. As my clothes fell in a puddle at my feet, I caught my reflection in the mirror. Not a single scar was visible.

I couldn't make my hands take my shirt off.

Layla appeared like an angel in my mind fog. "Let me help you." As she undid the buttons on my shirt, I watched her like I was in a dream.

She peeled open my shirt and as she slid it off my shoulders, she kissed my chest. I glided my hands over her wet shoulders and as I pushed her hair back, she kissed my left nipple then my right. The mist in the air failed to cool the inferno blazing through me.

She smelled amazing, all soap and fine, sexy woman. I smelled like crap.

If we didn't get into that shower soon, we were never going to. And Lord knew as much as I wanted to have sex with her, I needed a shower first.

Gripping her hand, I led her into the shower and turned her around so I couldn't get distracted by her glorious mouth, or amazing breasts, and the rest of her body that was demanding to be touched.

Maybe sensing my need to rid days of jungle grime off my flesh, she handed me a cake of soap.

As the hot shower cascaded over our wet bodies, I alternated scrubbing myself, and gliding the soap over Layla's soft, smooth skin. Every time I found a cut or a bruise, I scowled and kissed the wound that marred her delicate flesh.

I slid the soap over her shoulders and back, and she tilted her head, showing me the long line of her neck. She inched backward, and when my cock nudged her wet ass, I couldn't hold back a moment more. I turned her around.

"You drive me crazy, Layla." I crushed my lips to hers.

As I pushed my tongue into her mouth, tasting her, feeling her slick tongue press against mine, I explored her wet flesh with my hands, seeking her breasts. I cupped her perfect mounds, squeezing them and running my thumbs over her nipples that were as hard as pebbles.

A deep moan tumbled from her throat, and she seemed to melt toward me. I kissed her shoulder, her neck. In her ear, I whispered, "I missed you so much."

Layla flicked her gaze from my mouth to my eyes. Anticipation sizzled between us as I waited for her to reply, or scurry away.

"Oh, Hunter, I missed you too." Gripping my cheeks, she crushed her lips to mine.

Her tongue darted into my mouth, and it was the end of my self-control. Using my knee, I parted her legs, glided my hand up her slick inner thigh, and pushed my finger inside her.

"Oh yes. Yes." Her cries were loud, raw, and so fucking hot, I just about exploded.

Gritting my teeth, I drove my fingers into Layla's hot core, and she dragged her hands over my back. *Over my scars.* If she noticed, she didn't show it. I drove into her harder.

She cried out and as her entire body trembled, her hot juices pulsed around my fingers. As I watched my glorious woman succumb to primal bliss, years of pent-up frustration and anger melted away.

I was ready to give her everything I had to give: my body, my heart, and my soul.

She eased back and I soaked in how stunning she was. Her lips parted and her tongue lashed out like she was tasting me all over again.

"You're so beautiful, Layla."

She tilted her head, capturing me with her stunning eyes as she pulled me closer, and wrapped her hand around my cock.

I kissed her again, fierce and forceful, and as she glided her hand along my shaft, I groaned at her touch, so soft, yet so raw. Sucking air through my teeth, I said, "Careful, Layla. It's been a while."

She turned around, pressed her hands to the tiles, and angled her butt toward me. "I'm ready."

As warm water pounded my back, I slid my hands over her hips, feeling the gentle curve of her supple skin. She parted her legs and my cock throbbed to a primal beat as I guided my shaft into her hot zone.

She gasped as I drove every inch inside her until I was right up to my balls.

I paused there, feeling her hot flesh around my cock that was so stiff it hurt. My body was rock hard, primed, and ready. But I didn't want this moment to end. As soon as I moved, I was going to make a full assault on the glorious woman.

Layla peered at me over her shoulder. Her lips were parted. Her eyes were loaded with lust.

I hissed through clenched teeth. She was so fucking perfect.

She pushed her ass toward me adjusting her angle so she could drive my cock deeper into her hot zone.

Clutching her hips, I dragged my cock out and pounded back inside her. My rhythm was fast, deep, and hard as I rammed into her over and over. Her hot juices spilling around me was my undoing, and I could barely hold back.

When Layla cried out, a powerful orgasm ripped through me and I exploded, ramming myself into her core until I couldn't thrust any more.

I curled my arms around her body, pulling her back to my chest, and glided my hands over her wet flesh.

She rested her hands over mine. "I love you."

I kissed her neck. "I love you too."

Layla turned around and peered at me with so much love in her eyes I just about melted.

"Now," she said, placing her hand on my chest, "would you like me to wash your back?"

I cringed, but at the same time, my scars were like an elephant in the room. For us to be a couple who shared everything and held no secrets, I needed to let her look at my body.

"Hunter, your scars aren't your enemy."

I frowned at her.

"Your scars prove that you're a survivor. You lived through hell, and you're still a strong, brave, amazing man. They only define you if you let them."

"Huh, I thought you were a botanist, not a therapist."

She giggled. "I can be whatever you want me to be. But for now, I'm your nurse. Turn around."

Inhaling a deep breath, I turned my back to her, and as the shower pounded into my chest, Layla glided her warm hands over my back. She planted kisses over the jagged raised ribbons that threaded from my shoulder to my right butt cheek.

"Do they hurt?" she asked.

"Not at the moment."

"But they do sometimes," she said. "I see it in your eyes."

"Layla, you're ruining my sponge bath."

She smacked my butt. "I'll give you sponge bath, mister."

"Yes, please." I turned off the taps, scooped her

into my arms and dripping wet, I carried her to my bed.

We made love again, slow and fucking amazing. Our bodies moved in perfect harmony, each caress and kiss fueling the passion we shared. But this wasn't just sex. This was a true connection, one that came from the depths of my soul.

I have never felt so alive in my life.

Afterward, Layla dressed in a pair of my sweatpants and T-shirt. Holy hell, she looked hot and if it wasn't for my grumbling stomach, I would have stripped those clothes off her and made love to her again.

We headed out to the back deck with my stunning views over the Yellowstone mountains, and as I cooked our steaks on the barbeque, Layla played with Luna.

They seemed to forge an instant bond. Luna had been like that with me too. Maybe she'd sensed that I was scarred like her, and that was why she trusted me from the moment I took her from the bastard who owned her before me.

"How old is she?" Layla scratched behind Luna's ear.

"Not sure. The vet said she's about eight." I flipped over the steaks. "Looks like you've made a new friend."

"She's adorable. I've never had a dog before." Layla sighed and an intense sadness washed over her.

"What's wrong?"

Uncertainty flickered in her eyes as she scooped Luna onto her lap and looked across at Yellowstone mountains where the sunset cast a warm glow over the landscape.

"I was just wondering what the hell I'm going to do with myself now. I don't have a home. Or a car. Or a career."

I turned off the grill and sat beside her, flicking Luna off her lap. "You can stay here."

"Hunter—"

"I mean it, Layla. We've wasted too many years being apart. We have some serious catching up to do."

She curled her lip into her mouth. "Really? Are you sure?"

"Absolutely."

"Thank you." She leaned her head on my shoulder. "I'm going to enjoy watching this view every day."

"It's incredible, isn't it?"

"Yes, but I can't do that all day long. I need to find a job."

"Well . . . I have an idea."

"Oh yeah?" She sat up.

"After I left the hospital, I went to Brighter Days Rehab Ranch, which is run by an amazing woman named Hannah. I bet she'd be interested in your natural remedies."

Layla's eyes brightened. "Do you think so?"

"I think it's worth having a conversation with her."

"Thanks, Hunter." She heaved a sigh. "But before I do anything, I need to go to Blakely Pharmaceuticals."

"Do you want me to come with you?"

She shook her head.

"Well, don't you let them give you any shit. You face them head-on and tell them what that bastard Neville did."

"Don't worry, I will. Cody will support me."

"And we'll help you. Not just me, but everyone at Team Eagle. I'm certain Wyatt will get the data off your computer and Neville's that can help prove what he was doing."

She seemed to relax. "That would be amazing. Thanks. You guys are incredible."

"Anything for you, Layla."

Tears pooled in her eyes as she pressed her lips against mine. Our kiss was tender and filled with so much emotion, she seemed to melt into me.

As we eased apart, she whispered, "I love you. You truly have saved me."

The truth was, Layla had saved me. I had been a broken man, wallowing in self-pity. Now I could take on the world. My scars and pain were no longer going to define me. And in the Amazon I'd proven that I could still do anything I put my mind to.

My scars were part of me, and with Layla at my side, everything was perfect.

It was time to make everything perfect for Layla.

I knew exactly how I could help, but I was certain she would resist my idea, so I had to make it happen without telling her.

I just hoped my plan didn't backfire.

CHAPTER 18

LAYLA

One week later

I COULDN'T WIPE the smile off my face as I drove Hunter's truck back to his place. My meeting at Brighter Days Rehab Ranch had gone much better than I'd imagined, and as I pulled into Hunter's driveway, I spotted him in the dog training arena.

He waved at me and led Pistol, the new Belgian Shepherd he was training, into his pen.

He strode toward me as I jumped out of the truck. "And . . .?" His beaming smile added more joy to my morning.

"Hannah loved my idea."

He scooped me up and twirled me around. "I told you she would."

"She seemed as excited about using natural remedies to help the soldiers as I am. She listened to all my ideas and said she couldn't wait to see my work in action. I can't believe how interested she was."

"I can believe it. Drugs aren't always the answer."

He gripped my hand and as we strolled up the steps to his back deck, Luna came bounding out to us.

I scooped her into my arms. "Hello there. Have you been a good girl?"

As Luna licked the back of my hand, I glanced at the clock in the kitchen. "Wow, I didn't realize I'd been gone so long."

"I know. I was about to send another search party out for you." Grinning, he plucked a champagne bottle from the fridge. "Shall we celebrate?"

"It's a bit early . . . but okay." I giggled.

"It's never too early to celebrate." He popped the cork, but when he looked at me, an element of mischief blossomed in his eyes.

"What are you up to?" I said.

"Don't be mad at me."

The back kitchen counter held a prepared cheese platter.

"Why? Who's coming over?" I asked.

His brow knitted together. "Your sister."

"Sophia? But, but how did you . . .?"

He shrugged.

"It wasn't hard to find her and she's so excited to see you." He grabbed my shoulders and directed me toward the hallway. "Go get into some comfy clothes. She'll be here any minute."

As I strolled down the hallway, I didn't know whether to be mad at him for organizing this behind my back or thrilled to be seeing my sister after more than a year.

Truth was, I was both. But she's going to be really mad at me when I tell her where I've been.

I dressed in a Bohemian dress that I'd found at the op shop the other day and layered on a couple of beaded necklaces. It was nice to be in normal clothes again after spending eleven months in gumboots and long-sleeved shirts.

The sound of car tires popping on the gravel driveway made my heart race. I peered out the window as Hunter greeted Sophia. They gave each other a hug and were so comfortable together that I realized this meeting must have taken some planning between them.

Laughing despite my annoyance at him going behind my back, I raced up the hallway and out the front door.

"Sophia," I called as I ran to her.

We wrapped our arms around each other.

"Layla. It's so good to see you."

Hunter helped the two kids out of the back of the car.

"Oh my gosh, haven't you two grown." I kneeled

down and gave Oliver and Grace a hug. "Hello, guys, I've missed you."

"Where did you go, Aunty Layla?" Grace captured me with her big blue eyes.

"I went to the jungle!"

Oliver gasped. "The jungle? Did you see any snakes?"

As Hunter led Sophia into the house, Oliver and Grace gripped my hands and bombarded me with a dozen questions.

Hunter started the barbeque and as the kids played with Luna, Sophia and I caught up on our year apart.

"I can't believe you went to the Amazon without telling me," Sophia said.

I glared at Hunter; he'd obviously told her. "What?" He shrugged. "You didn't tell me either. Sophia and I compared notes," Hunter said.

I scowled at him. "I didn't tell you because I knew you'd try to stop me. *And* you, Sophia. I knew you wouldn't want me to go."

Sophia frowned. "No, that's not true. I'd support you no matter what you planned to do. "Do Mom and Dad know you're back?" Sophia asked.

"Not yet. I wanted to have a few things sorted before I saw them. You know, like a job, and where I'm going to live. You know how they worry."

"They're still going to be mad at you. They thought you were in Brazil," Sophia said.

"Well, technically, I was in Brazil. Just in the Amazon Jungle region."

Sophia chuckled and gave me a 'good luck with that' look. "Why did you go to the Amazon Jungle? What did you do down there?"

As Hunter kept our glasses topped up and looked after the barbeque, I told Sophia about my research trip.

"A burn ointment? Oh, Layla, don't tell me you did that because of what happened all those years ago."

Sucking my lips into my mouth, I nodded.

"You crazy woman, you risked your life because of that? Because of me?"

"Because of what I did to you." I indicated toward her left leg, which was still covered in nasty, red scars that looked about a month old, not fourteen years old.

"You didn't do anything to me. It was a silly accident." She reached for my hand and squeezed. "You need to stop this before you kill yourself. I have never blamed you for what happened, so there was no need to forgive you. All I want . . ." She swept her hand toward the kids who were running around on the grass with Luna. "All *we* want is you in our lives. That's what matters, Layla. Not some ointment."

"Well said." Hunter filled our glasses with more champagne.

"Don't you start, mister. You're still in trouble for organizing this without my knowledge."

"Don't be mad at Hunter," Sophia said. "Because of him, I have my sister back in my life and my kids have their aunty. We're a family again."

I grinned at Hunter. "Yes. Yes, we are."

As the weight of my relief lifted from my shoulders, I knew I'd found the man of my dreams. A man who knew me, who understood me, and accepted me.

A man who would support me no matter what I did.

As long as it didn't involve wild trips to the Amazon Jungle.

THE END

Team EAGLE
Booker's Mission - Kris Norris
Hunter's Mission - Kendall Talbot
Gunn's Mission - Delilah Devlin
Xavier's Mission - Lori Matthews
Wyatt's Mission - Jen Talty

BROTHERHOOD PROTECTORS

ORIGINAL SERIES BY ELLE JAMES

Bayou Brotherhood Protectors

Remy (#1)

Gerard (#2)

Lucas (#3)

Beau (#4)

Rafael (#5)

Valentin (#6)

Landry (#7)

Simon (#8)

Maurice (#9)

Jacques (#10)

Brotherhood Protectors Yellowstone

Saving Kyla (#1)

Saving Chelsea (#2)

Saving Amanda (#3)

Saving Liliana (#4)

Saving Breely (#5)

Saving Savvie (#6)

Saving Jenna (#7)

Saving Peyton (#8)

Brotherhood Protectors Colorado

SEAL Salvation (#1)

Rocky Mountain Rescue (#2)

Ranger Redemption (#3)

Tactical Takeover (#4)

Colorado Conspiracy (#5)

Rocky Mountain Madness (#6)

Free Fall (#7)

Colorado Cold Case (#8)

Fool's Folly (#9)

Colorado Free Rein (#10)

Rocky Mountain Venom (#11)

High Country Hero (#12)

Brotherhood Protectors

Montana SEAL (#1)

Bride Protector SEAL (#2)

Montana D-Force (#3)

Cowboy D-Force (#4)

Montana Ranger (#5)

Montana Dog Soldier (#6)

Montana SEAL Daddy (#7)

Montana Ranger's Wedding Vow (#8)

Montana SEAL Undercover Daddy (#9)

Cape Cod SEAL Rescue (#10)

Montana SEAL Friendly Fire (#11)

Montana SEAL's Mail-Order Bride (#12)

SEAL Justice (#13)

Ranger Creed (#14)

Delta Force Rescue (#15)

Dog Days of Christmas (#16)

Montana Rescue (#17)

Montana Ranger Returns (#18)

Hot SEAL Salty Dog (SEALs in Paradise)

Hot SEAL, Hawaiian Nights (SEALs in Paradise)

Hot SEAL Bachelor Party (SEALs in Paradise)

Hot SEAL, Independence Day (SEALs in Paradise)

Brotherhood Protectors Boxed Set 1

Brotherhood Protectors Boxed Set 2

Brotherhood Protectors Boxed Set 3

Brotherhood Protectors Boxed Set 4

Brotherhood Protectors Boxed Set 5

Brotherhood Protectors Boxed Set 6

ABOUT ELLE JAMES

ELLE JAMES also writing as MYLA JACKSON is a *New York Times* and *USA Today* Bestselling author of books including cowboys, intrigues and paranormal adventures that keep her readers on the edges of their seats. When she's not at her computer, she's traveling, snow skiing, boating, or riding her ATV, dreaming up new stories. Learn more about Elle James at www.ellejames.com

Website | Facebook | Twitter | GoodReads | Newsletter | BookBub | Amazon

Or visit her alter ego Myla Jackson at mylajackson.com
Website | Facebook | Twitter | Newsletter

Follow Me!
www.ellejames.com
ellejamesauthor@gmail.com

Printed in Great Britain
by Amazon